Elsie's
Great
Hope

Elsie's Great Hope

BOOK EIGHT

of the
*A Life of Faith:
Elsie Dinsmore*
Series

Based on the beloved books by
Martha Finley

MCP
Mission City Press

Franklin, Tennessee

Book Eight of the *A Life of Faith: Elsie Dinsmore* Series

Elsie's Great Hope
Copyright © 2001, Mission City Press, Inc. All Rights Reserved.

Published by Mission City Press, Inc.

This book is based on the *Elsie Dinsmore* books written by Martha Finley and first published in 1868 by Dodd, Mead & Company.

Cover & Interior Design: Richmond & Williams, Nashville, Tennessee
Cover Photography: Michelle Grisco Photography, West Covina, California
Typesetting: BookSetters, White House, Tennessee

Unless otherwise indicated, all Scripture references are from the Holy Bible, New International Version (NIV). Copyright © 1973, 1978, 1984 by International Bible Society. Used by permission of Zondervan Publishing House, Grand Rapids, MI. All rights reserved.

Elsie Dinsmore and *A Life of Faith* are trademarks of Mission City Press, Inc.

For more information, write to Mission City Press 202 Second Avenue South, Franklin, Tennessee 37064, or visit our Web Site at **www.alifeoffaith.com**.

For a FREE catalog call 1-800-840-2641.

Library of Congress Catalog Card Number: 00-107359
Finley, Martha
     Elsie's Great Hope
     Book Eight of the *A Life of Faith: Elsie Dinsmore* Series
     Hardcover: ISBN–10: 1-928749-08-9
                      ISBN–13: 978-1-928749-08-0
     Softcover: ISBN–10: 1-928749-87-9
                      ISBN–13: 978-1-928749-87-5

Printed in the United States of America
7 8 9 10 11— 11 10 09

DEDICATION

This book is
dedicated to
the memory of
MARTHA FINLEY

*May the rich legacy of
pure and simple devotion to Christ
that she introduced through
Elsie Dinsmore in 1868
live on in our day and
in generations to come.*

— FOREWORD —

*T*he story of *Elsie's Great Hope* begins a decade after the end of the American Civil War and will take readers through the nation's Centennial year — the hundredth year after the signing of the Declaration of Independence. Elsie's young family has grown in number, and a series of tragic events have brought others under the family's wings. It is a time of both sorrow and hope for the Travillas and Dinsmores. They will suffer loss and fear of loss, yet they will gain insights and experience the pleasures of family and friendships. Romance is also in the air, as a new generation enters adulthood.

Like all their fellow countrymen in the 1870s, the Travillas and the Dinsmores must have felt the excitement of America's expansion and the rise of new industries and opportunities. This was a period of tumultuous change for the nation and for the popular heroine of Miss Martha Finley's novels.

Readers today may wonder what made the Elsie novels so popular in their day. The fundamental reason, then and now, is that Miss Finley provided American children and adults with models of Christian faith in the context of daily living. Although Elsie Dinsmore Travilla enjoys privileges that few girls and women of her time would ever know, she must nevertheless face personal troubles and trials that are universal. Whatever their social and economic position, readers in the nineteenth century could identify with Elsie's difficulties and learn from and be inspired by her actions and reactions. As Elsie struggles to be a good daughter, wife, and mother, God is her constant friend and guide, and she is always willing to place her total trust in Him.

This underlying message is no less powerful and persuasive now than in the 1870s. Miss Finley understood that God's gifts to His children are eternal. In adapting the Elsie novels for modern readers, Mission City Press strives in every way to promote the timeless truths that Martha Finley espoused, to honor her faith and her work, and to carry her message forward so that it may give help and hope to readers of today and tomorrow.

ELSIE'S WORLD IN THE 1870S

The United States in the mid-1870s was a very different place from the country into which Elsie Dinsmore was born in the 1830s. The number of people in the country tripled in that time. In the official census of 1830, the number of Americans was slightly less than 13 million; by 1870, the count was approaching 39 million, and it exceeded 50 million in the 1880 census.

The country was enlarging geographically as well. In 1830, there were twenty-four states in the Union, with only Louisiana and Missouri extending west of the Mississippi River. By August of 1876, the number of states had grown to thirty-eight including California and Oregon on the edge of the Pacific Ocean, and the western territories were being settled rapidly. Another six states, all in the West and Northwest, would be added over the next twenty-five years.

The country was also growing in terms of opportunity. In 1830, the vast majority of workers were employed in agriculture. But by 1870, the range of jobs available was enormous, and the chance to make a good living or even a fortune seemed open to all hard-working men. (Women, African-Americans, and Native Americans were excluded by law and tradition from this aspect of the American Dream.) Immigrants — most of them from European countries — poured into the U.S. in the hope of making better lives for themselves and their children.

The country needed workers to man its new iron and steel mills, build its railroads, manufacture its clothing, till its fields and process its food, mine its coal and other natural resources, herd its cattle, and so on. American workers were not usually well paid, but jobs were plentiful, and Americans were driven by a strong work ethic. If the mine owners and railroad builders took advantage of their workers through poor pay and dangerous working conditions, the workers themselves cherished the notion that they might someday rise up the ladder of success and achieve wealth and power. A lucky few — like Andrew Carnegie, a poor Scottish immigrant who started working at age thirteen and became the richest steel manufacturer in the world — did live out the dream and became role models for their ambitious countrymen.

Some were excluded from the dream. African-Americans in the South lost their hope for real equality with the end of Reconstruction and were deliberately kept in poverty and ignorance. As white Americans moved westward, Native American Indians were driven from their lands and deprived of their livelihoods, traditions, and cultures. Over decades of bloody conflict, the Native American peoples saw their numbers reduced and their freedoms virtually eliminated as they were pushed into reservations overseen by corrupt government agencies and officials. Women, whatever their color, had access to few of the opportunities open to men, but more and more women were speaking up and demanding legal and economic equality. Education for girls and young women was becoming a rallying cry for the mothers and daughters of the country, and slowly but surely women began to enter the traditional male professions of medicine, law, and religious ministry.

The idea that all children should be sent to school was just beginning to take root. By the middle 1870s, all states provided some level of public elementary school education and were debating and passing laws that required school attendance. Public high schools were growing in number, and under a law called the Morrill Act, the federal government gave large tracts of land to each state for the establishment of colleges of agriculture and mechanical arts. (Many of today's great public universities evolved from these land-grant colleges.) But not everyone benefited from such educational opportunities. Poor children were often sent to work in factories and on farms before they reached their teens. Children were valued as workers because they were paid much less than adults, and there were no legal restrictions on the hours they could work and the health and safety of their workplaces. For impoverished families, there was often no choice but to put their children to work.

New Ideas — The last half of the nineteenth century was an age of innovation and invention. Many of the conveniences that people now take for granted were first developed during those decades. Almost simultaneously, British inventor Joseph Swan and America's Thomas A. Edison hit upon the idea of an incandescent light bulb powered by electricity, patenting their inventions in 1878 and 1879 respectively. It took some years for the electric light to become more than a curiosity, but it is hard to imagine life today without the humble light bulb. Our comfortable central heating systems evolved from the coal-burning and then steam-producing furnaces that warmed middle- and upper-class homes in Elsie's day. Indoor plumbing was introduced into many homes, including piped water, bath-tubs, and "water closets" (flush toilets). Mothers in the 1870s cooked on wood or coal-burning "ranges," which allowed the preparation of more varied meals than the old method of cooking over open fires.

The growth of American manufacturing meant that many new products were available to American consumers. For example, a family with a good income could buy packaged soap instead of making their own, though people continued to make many of their household materials including tooth powder, shampoo, cleansers, and polishes. (Detergents were not invented until the 1890s.) Cosmetics of the type used today were not available, but mothers and daughters followed family recipes to create their own face and hand creams, hairdressings, and perfumes. The sewing machine had been used for some time, but in the 1870s, the new knitting machine helped add to a family's wardrobe. And steam-powered washing machines with wringers eased the labor of wash day.

Keeping a house clean was an endless and backbreaking job, but the invention of the mechanical carpet sweeper by Anna and Melville Bissell of Michigan was considered a revolution in housekeeping. (Even Queen Victoria of England ordered Bissell sweepers for her palace.) Linoleum flooring, a British invention, fascinated visitors to the 1876 Philadelphia Exhibition and promised an end to the dirty, daily chore of washing and sweeping rough wood floors. Since most people could not afford to pay for such expensive products outright, a new kind of buying was developed — the installment plan by which people paid for items over a period of time, much like our modern credit cards.

Advertising for such innovations was everywhere, as sellers touted the virtues of their wares in newspapers and magazines and on billboards. Not all new products were what they claimed, however, especially in the area of health remedies. Americans had learned to associate dirt and dust with illness, but as yet they did not know about germs and bacteria. Soldiers in the Civil War were often treated for diseases such as dysentery and typhoid with nonprescription medicines called "patent medicines," and the country as a whole turned to these commercial remedies with zest after the war. The makers of tonics, syrups, poultices, and healing devices made extravagant promises and sometimes associated their products with Indian remedies, which Americans tended to trust. The medicine show — a kind of traveling outdoor performance whose purpose was to peddle medicines — was a welcome entertainment in rural and western towns. Almanacs filled with ads for remedies were published by medicine-makers and distributed to millions of homes. Advertisements called "picture cards" were handed out by druggists and eagerly collected by children like today's sports trading cards. Unfortunately, most of the bottled medicines and healing devices had little or no curative value, and some were actually harmful. Many contained high concentrations of alcohol and narcotic substances. The medicines "worked" because the alcohol and drugs made people feel better, not because they had any health benefits.

Still, many nineteenth century inventions and technologies did deliver on their promises to make life better. Among the items and devices that were invented, developed, or popularized in this period were hand-pushed lawn mowers, rubber garden hoses and fire hoses, ready-mixed paints, paper bags, safety matches, toilet paper, photo film, can openers, filter coffeepots, vacuum thermos bottles, aluminum cookware, dishwashers, safety razors, and metal zippers. Potato chips, graham crackers, cracker jacks, and chewing gum are just a few of the edibles we have inherited from the nineteenth century, along with clothing items including blue jeans, dress tuxedo suits, and zippers. Even printed Christmas cards come from the nineteenth century.

It's hard to imagine America without baseball, football, and basketball — sports that were formalized and enjoyed by young men in the 1800s. Girls, however, were discouraged from most sporting activities, though with the invention of steel blades, ice-skating was considered suitably ladylike. Adventurous girls might try activities like rowing, fishing, and bicycle riding, so long as they weren't seen by disapproving elders. Even so sedate a game as croquet, played by men and children, was considered improper for women in their long skirts. Sports were divided along class lines as well: poor people bowled, for example, and rich people played golf. But whatever the sport and the restrictions, a great many ordinary Americans in the second half of the nineteenth century at last had the necessary free time to enjoy leisure activities.

Elsie's Great Hope

Real Problems — Despite the many new conveniences and improvements, life was not easy for most Americans. The cities of the eastern states were growing as people sought employment in manufacturing. In major cities like New York, poor people were forced to live in over-crowded housing and could not afford decent medical treatment, even when it was available. The pressures on city services such as water and sewer systems, transportation, and fire-fighting services were often more than city leaders could handle. Fatal fires and outbreaks of diseases due to poor sanitation were all too common. Because there were no laws regulating workplaces, accidents were frequent, yet employers usually felt no obligation to pay for the care of their injured workers or provide support for the families of workers who died.

With the growth of business and industry, the gap between rich and poor widened. The last half of the nine-teenth century saw the beginning of labor movements to protect workers and of social movements to improve the lives of the poor and of children in particular. It was not until the twentieth century, however, that these efforts achieved real reform for poor and working-class Americans.

In the early 1870s, the country faced a series of events that shook Americans' faith in their government and their economy. The federal government was rocked by financial scandals that involved members of Congress and some of the highest-ranking officials of President Ulysses S. Grant's Cabinet, though the President himself was not implicated. News of corrupt financial dealings and bribery schemes undermined the confidence of ordinary citizens in their leaders. Adding to the country's troubles was the economic panic of 1873, followed by four years of depression. The country's rapid growth after the Civil War had led businessmen and bankers to believe that the boom was limitless, and they took no precautions against less affluent times.

The bubble burst with the collapse of a leading investment firm in 1873, and within a year, business failures were rampant. The early failures were mainly in the railroad companies, but an economic depression is like a house of cards — when one card falls, the rest will follow. Businesses of all types were ruined. Some three million workers lost their jobs, and those who held on to their jobs saw their wages plummet. Agriculture was drastically affected when prices for farm goods dropped so low that thousands of farmers were forced to abandon their land. The depression lasted for four years and was one of the worst the country has ever endured.

In the midst of scandal and hard times, Americans were anxious for something that would raise their spirits. One of the answers was the celebration of the country's first hundred years of independence and the mounting of a great international exhibition in the birthplace of American democracy — Philadelphia, Pennsylvania.

∽ THE CENTENNIAL EXHIBITION ∽

Philadelphia's Centennial Exhibition, held from May 10 through November 10, 1876, was the country's most important display of its history and progress to date. The official name of the fair — The International Exhibition of Arts, Manufactures, and Products of the Soil and Mine — reflected Americans' new sense of their importance in the world. The motto of the fair — "1776 with 3 million people on a strip of seacoast; 1876 with 40 million people from ocean to ocean" — summarized the country's growth both in size and in population.

Centennial celebrations were held in villages, towns, and cities across the country, but none outdid the Philadelphia Exhibition. It had not been easy to raise funds for the construction of the fair, and many exhibits were not finished on opening day. Financial problems plagued the fair's organizers from start to finish, and for a variety of reasons, attendance was not as high as expected. Still, over six months an estimated 10 million visitors paid the entry fee of fifty cents to attend the huge display of American pride and power.

President Grant and his wife arrived at Fairmount Park, the site of the fair located about four miles from the center of the city, on the morning of the first day as a crowd of almost 200,000 people jostled to get a view of the ceremonies. It had rained the day before, and the grounds were muddy, but no one seemed to care. A grand orchestra played patriotic songs, and fair officials made the usual long-winded speeches (mostly unheard since there were no such things as loudspeakers and public address systems yet). Then the President stepped forward and with a few brief remarks, he declared the Exhibition officially open.

Although many of the agricultural and manufacturing exhibits were boring even by the standards of the day, there were plenty of thrills and spectacular sights. Visitors could stand 185 feet above ground atop the Sawyer Observatory; ride the Prismoidal Railway for Rapid Transit, an early monorail; and stand in awe before the mighty Corliss engine (named for its builder, George Henry Corliss), the world's largest steam engine, which powered all the machinery in the Exhibition. A narrow-gauge steam railroad transported visitors to main buildings around the park, but many thought its eight-miles-per-hour speed shockingly fast. The "largest statue of modern times" towered over fair-goers outside the main exhibit hall. In August, fair-goers were treated to a new spectacle when the copper arm, hand, and flaming torch of the Statue of Liberty were assembled on the fairground. Onlookers were astonished by this display, which would someday top the completed statue in New York Harbor — the gift of the people of France to the people of the United States.

Some of the displays stirred controversy. When some visitors were outraged by the lifelike movements of a colorful, mechanized wax sculpture of Cleopatra with a slave girl and a fluttering parrot, the exhibit was removed from public view. Equally shocking were some statues from Europe that were eventually placed in a little-visited area of the Art Museum. But the biggest controversy involved the decision of Exhibition directors not to open the fair on Sundays. Employees at the time worked full six-day weeks, and employers were unlikely to grant days off to visit the fair. Despite loud protests that the Sunday closing deprived ordinary working people of their chance to see the exhibition, the officials maintained the Sabbath day ban.

From Monday through Saturday, however, families could enjoy exhibits from across the U.S. and other countries. Since traveling the world was beyond the budgets of all but the wealthy, many visitors got their first exposure to foreign cultures and customs in the displays sent by England, France, Italy, Germany, the Scandinavian countries, Russia, Turkey, Egypt, China, and others. What fair-goers saw in the

Japanese house actually changed the way many Americans decorated their own homes. The Japanese-style décor was very simple and sparse — in marked contrast to cluttered American interiors in the Victorian era — and inspired thousands of middle-class homemakers to simplify their own home design.

Equally exciting were the two dozen state buildings erected around "States Avenue." Here, families could see a Mississippi bark log cabin, artifacts from Paul Revere and John Alden in the Old Colony House of Massachusetts, and a Quaker lady demonstrating an antique spinning wheel in Pennsylvania's exhibit. Meals were plentiful and affordable in places such as the Southern Restaurant. An exception was a French restaurant called Les Tres Freres Provencaux (The Three Brothers of Provence). The editor of the *Atlantic Monthly* magazine, writer William Dean Howells, speculated that the meals were so costly there because each of the three brothers charged separately. But on the fair grounds, visitors could cool off with glasses of lemonade and root beer and ice cream sodas sold for a few pennies or the free iced water at the Catholic Total Abstinence Fountain. Children particularly enjoyed the red, white, and blue popcorn balls and bananas sold in tin foil wrappers, but peanuts were not allowed in the fairgrounds because officials dreaded cleaning up the shells each night. Food was also on display in grand scale — a 15-foot-tall cathedral made of spun sugar, a 200-pound vase of pure chocolate, a Grecian statue carved from butter.

As Howells noted in his article about the Exhibition, the most significant American contribution was "the superior elegance, aptness, and ingenuity of our machinery . . . . Yes, it is still in these things of iron and steel that the national genius most freely speaks . . . . " The Machinery Hall indeed drew the most attention, for the gigantic Corliss engine and powerful machines that produced great quantities of pins, chewing tobacco, newspapers, and other products. But people were also amazed by smaller inventions including the typewriter and the Otis Elevator. Another recent invention initially drew few interested observers, although it would soon change the lives of all Americans. It was the telephone, demonstrated by its inventor, Alexander Graham Bell.

Another display that was to profoundly affect the way Americans worked and played was the English "ordinary" bicycle. Although it was of the large front wheel type, this exhibit sparked interest that would eventually become a national obsession with cycling. When the British introduced the "safety" bicycle (two wheels of equal size like modern bikes) nine years later, the craze was set in motion, and historians credit the popularity of bicycles with paving the way for the motor car at the end of the nineteenth century.

The Women's Pavilion, funded entirely by American women, featured countless items produced by women, from household goods and clothing to manufactured products. A female engineer ran the machinery that provided power for the Pavilion. Though the Pavilion managers had had to go to Canada to find a qualified woman engineer, her presence inspired many girls and young women with thoughts of careers outside the traditional role of housewife.

In spite of its problems and financial losses, the Philadelphia Exhibition was generally deemed a great success. On November 10, three days after the unresolved presidential election of 1876, President Grant made his way back to Philadelphia to turn off the Corliss engine and bring the fair to its close. It was a wet, cold day, but visitors gathered to hear speeches and join together to sing "America."

The fair had been criticized as tacky and tasteless by famous Americans including philosopher William James and humorist Mark Twain, yet observers also praised its exuberance and diversity. Without much fanfare, the Exhibition had attracted international men of science who heard, among other lecturers, Joseph Lister speak of his "germ theory" and the need for antiseptic surgery — ideas that would transform medical practice before the end of the century. Information shared at the fair, including news about smallpox vaccination, led to improvements in life for all Americans. Perhaps most important at the time, the Exhibition had boosted America's flagging spirits and promoted a national sense of self-confidence. As William Dean Howells wrote after his visit to Fairmount Park, "No one can now see the fair without a thrill of patriotic pride." When the hum of the Corliss engine faded away, those who had attended and those who had only read about the Philadelphia Exhibition were left with a better understanding of their history and renewed trust in the future progress and possibilities of their nation.

DINSMORE FAMILY TREE

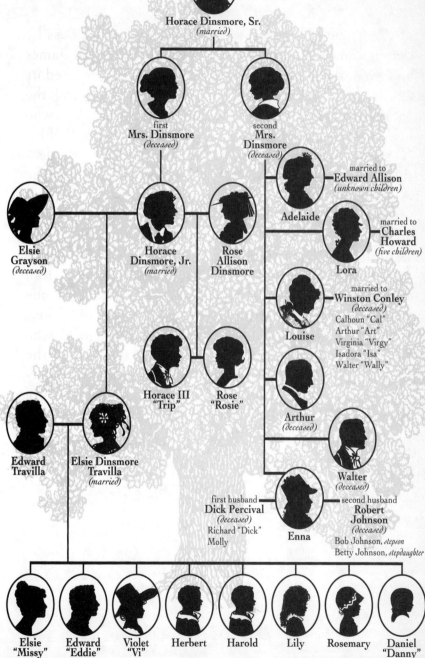

Horace Dinsmore, Sr.
(married)

first
Mrs. Dinsmore
(deceased)

second
Mrs. Dinsmore
(deceased)

Elsie Grayson
(deceased)

Horace Dinsmore, Jr.
(married)

Rose Allison Dinsmore

Adelaide
married to
Edward Allison
(unknown children)

Lora
married to
Charles Howard
(five children)

Louise
married to
Winston Conley
(deceased)
Calhoun "Cal"
Arthur "Art"
Virginia "Virgy"
Isadora "Isa"
Walter "Wally"

Horace III "Trip"

Rose "Rosie"

Arthur
(deceased)

Edward Travilla

Elsie Dinsmore Travilla
(married)

Walter
(deceased)

first husband
Dick Percival
(deceased)
Richard "Dick"
Molly

Enna

second husband
Robert Johnson
(deceased)
Bob Johnson, *stepson*
Betty Johnson, *stepdaughter*

Elsie "Missy"

Edward "Eddie"

Violet "Vi"

Herbert

Harold

Lily

Rosemary

Daniel "Danny"

SETTING

𝒯he story begins in the early autumn of 1874 in the South.

CHARACTERS

∽ ION ∾

Elsie Dinsmore Travilla, the wealthy daughter of Horace Dinsmore, Jr.

Edward Travilla, Elsie's husband and owner of Ion

Their children:

> **Elsie ("Missy"), age 17**
> **Edward ("Eddie"), age 15**
> **Violet ("Vi"), age 11**
> **Herbert and Harold, the twins,** age 9
> **Lily, age 6**
> **Rosemary, age 4**
> **Daniel ("Danny"),** the baby

Aunt Chloe — Elsie's faithful nursemaid, friend, and companion

Old Joe — Chloe's elderly husband

Mr. and Mrs. Daly — the new tutor and housekeeper

Ben — Edward's valet

Christine — nursemaid to Rosemary and Danny

∽ THE OAKS ∾

Horace Dinsmore, Jr. — Elsie's father, owner of The Oaks plantation

Rose Allison Dinsmore — his second wife

Their children:

> **Horace, III ("Trip")**, age 27
> **Rose ("Rosie")**, age 20

∾ ROSELANDS ∾

Horace Dinsmore, Sr. — Elsie's grandfather, a widower, owner of Roselands

Louise Dinsmore Conley, widowed daughter of Horace, Sr., and her children:

> **Calhoun ("Cal)**, age 26
> **Arthur ("Art")**, age 22
> **Virginia ("Virgy")**, age 20
> **Isadora ("Isa")**, age 18
> **Walter ("Wally")**, age 17

Enna Dinsmore Percival Johnson, twice-widowed daughter of Horace, Sr., and her children and stepchildren:

> **Richard ("Dick") Percival**, age 21
> **Molly Percival**, age 18
> **Bob Johnson**, age 12
> **Betty Johnson**, age 11

∾ FAIRVIEW ∾

John and Mary Leland — Northerners who own Fairview plantation

Lester Leland — their nephew, an artist

∾ OTHERS ∾

The **Allison family** of Philadelphia — parents and siblings of Rose Dinsmore

The **Carringtons** of Ashlands plantation — long-time friends of the Dinsmores and Travillas

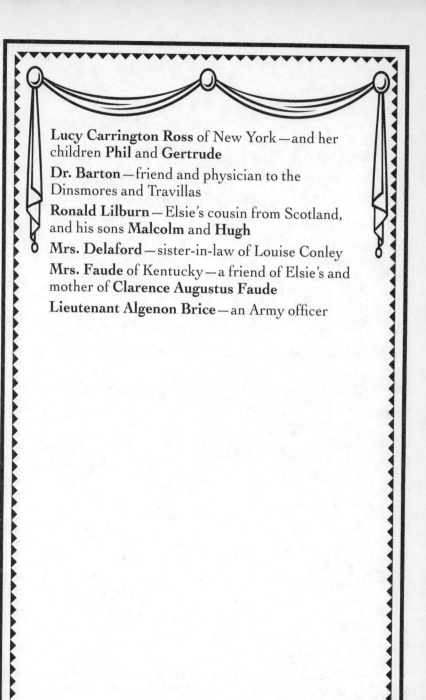

Lucy Carrington Ross of New York — and her children **Phil** and **Gertrude**

Dr. Barton — friend and physician to the Dinsmores and Travillas

Ronald Lilburn — Elsie's cousin from Scotland, and his sons **Malcolm** and **Hugh**

Mrs. Delaford — sister-in-law of Louise Conley

Mrs. Faude of Kentucky — a friend of Elsie's and mother of **Clarence Augustus Faude**

Lieutenant Algenon Brice — an Army officer

CHAPTER

1

A Writer's Journal

In the beginning was

the Word . . .

JOHN 1:1

A Writer's Journal

First entry in the personal journal of Molly Percival, dated September 21, 1874:

I have resolved to be a writer.

How easy it is now to put that sentence upon this fresh sheet of paper! Yet my journey to this point has been difficult and painful to both body and soul. Most people would say that I should put my troubled past behind me and get on with living. But a writer has just one unfailing source of inspiration from which to draw, and that is her own experience. So I set out on the path I have chosen by beginning this journal. Here, I shall commit what I know of the past and what I see of life in the future. And I will start, as writers often do, with my own story.

My name is Molly Percival. People who do not know me are surely tempted to pity me, and there was a time not long ago when I pitied myself most of all. Five years ago, I suffered a loss that seemed unbearably cruel. But wait — I shall tell the story as it occurred, not as the heroine of my own tale, but as objectively as I can. For if I am to be a writer, then I must learn the discipline of my craft.

When I was fourteen, I was living at Roselands, the house of my grandfather. I had no father, for my own Papa was killed in the war, and my stepfather, whom I recall through a child's misty memory, was also lost in that terrible conflict. So I lived at Roselands with my mother and my brother, Dick, and my stepbrother and stepsister, Bob and Betty. I did not understand then the responsibility that my

Grandpapa had accepted. His own losses during the war — a wife and two sons — might have made him bitter and inclined to retreat into the solitude of his grief. Yet he opened his home to my family and also to my Aunt Louise, herself a war widow, and her five children.

My mother is Grandpapa's youngest child. To this day, he sometimes calls her "Pet," for that is what she was — the baby of the family, petted, and spoiled by one and all. If I am to be clear-eyed about my story, I must concede that my mother, Enna, never outgrew her childhood. Oh, she grew tall and very pretty and witty in her way, yet the maturity of womanhood eluded her. She retained the liveliness of a girl, and the faults of pampered youth as well. In a way, I think of her still as my vivacious but self-centered and frivolous playmate. She was never prepared to be a mother, for motherhood requires selflessness. And back then, I had not the temperament to be a dutiful and obedient child.

I can see now that what I am today began on a spring day in 1869. The residents of Roselands had been invited to a picnic at the home of my Cousin Elsie, and Mamma was, as always, determined that we should make an appearance every bit as fine as that of my wealthy cousin and her children. Mamma and a maid spent what seemed like hours dressing me for the event. First this dress, then that dress, then another until Mamma was satisfied. No argument on my part made a dent in her determination. Sashes were tied and retied. My hair was brushed and pinned up with heavy combs, then brushed again and braided, then unbraided and beribboned. Nothing would do but perfection, and the more I protested (which I did without restraint), the more Mamma demanded.

Having rigged me from head to ankle, she decided that I must be shod in the latest fashion. She had purchased for me a pair of gaiter boots, which laced prettily but rose on high, thin heels that made walking treacherous. I preferred my comfortable black leather boots, which had very little heel. I stamped my foot in protest and shouted that I hated the gaiters and that the heels were dangerous — Grandpapa and Dr. Barton both said so. Mamma would not hear me. She just remarked that the boots would make my feet look so dainty. Then she said I must wear them or stay at home. I might have continued my battle with Mamma over the footwear, but at that moment, Dick knocked upon my bedroom door and called out that Grandpapa was waiting in the carriage. The prospect of the picnic at Ion proved a stronger attraction than another argument with Mamma. So I slipped on the high-heeled boots, and the maid laced them while Mamma pinned my straw hat to my hair — repositioning it several times before she was happy with its jaunty angle.

Released at last, I hurried from my room to the stairway that led downstairs. The shoes were most uncooperative, and I was in too much of a hurry. I did not even pause at the top of the stairs but stepped down quickly as was my usual habit. There was, I was told later, a worn place in the carpet that covered the stairs, so small it could hardly be seen, and my elegant heel was caught by one of the loose fibers.

I remember the fall all too vividly — my one foot suddenly resisting any further movement, my other foot slipping away beneath me, and the sensation for an instant in time that I had come unloosed from the ground and was truly flying. I reached for the banister but could not right myself and plunged headlong. And there my memory fails. Dick, who was standing in the hallway below, has said that he had the impression of a bundle of white clothing cascading down the steps. I did not cry out, he says, and it was only when I reached the bottom that he realized the bundle was his own sister. He felt strangely relieved to hear me moaning and instantly called out for help. Two servants came, followed by Grandpapa, who instructed that I be moved from the floor to the large sofa in the parlor. I remember none of this. When I came back to consciousness, Mamma was sitting beside me, and the odor of her smelling salts remains with me still. I saw that Grandpapa was there, too, and Dick — his face as pale as this paper — and Cousin Cal.

"Such foolishness," Mamma was saying, "to insist on wearing those high boots. There, she is awake. Molly dear, are you hurt?"

"Of course, she's hurt," Grandpapa said gruffly. "She has fallen down a flight of stairs. We must send for Dr. Barton."

Grandpapa added his opinion that no bones were broken, but a fall must be taken seriously. And then I spoke, telling them all that I was fine, although my back hurt somewhat.

At that, Mamma stood up and said, "You hear? She is well." And I, believing the dull pain would go away, agreed. My head was clear now, and the vision of the picnic dominated my thoughts. I tried to raise myself, but the pain stopped me, and my legs seemed unwilling to move at my command. I sank back against the pillow.

Then Cal, so recently returned to us, spoke up. He insisted that I not be moved again, that the doctor be summoned immediately, and that the rest of the family should go on to Ion. He would stay with me and Mamma.

I saw the look of disappointment on my mother's face, though she quickly altered her expression to one of concern and said, "If Molly wishes me to stay, then of course, I shall remain here at her side."

"No, Mamma, I want you go to Cousin Elsie's," I said. It was not, to be truthful, a selfless desire. I simply could not bear to be the object of Mamma's accusations. I knew that she would, in her way, hold me accountable for the accident and her missing the picnic. My awkwardness, my carelessness, my lack of "feminine" graces — all my failings and flaws would be examined minutely if she were forced to nurse me.

Grandpapa required rather more convincing, and Dick — sweet Dick with tears trembling in his eyes — demanded to stay at my side, until I insisted that he go and asked him to bring back for me some of Cousin Elsie's delicious buns and tea cakes. But at last they departed, and a servant was dispatched to find Dr. Barton. Cal remained with me, telling me stories of his time in Philadelphia and of our Aunt Adelaide and all the Allisons until I drifted off to sleep.

I will not detail the remainder of that day or the many days and weeks that followed. It is enough to say that I have not walked since. The injury to my back was graver than anyone had suspected. My spine was damaged beyond all hope of repair. I need not record the names of all the physicians who have examined me, including the great specialist in Philadelphia who confirmed all their opinions. It is enough to write that I will not walk again.

How calmly I can make that statement now. Yet how desperately I fought the doctors' verdict. I would not — could not — believe them. I was fourteen years old, a girl at the gate of adulthood. How could my life have come to an end? Truly I regarded my crippled state as a kind of living death that had snatched all hope of happiness from me. I cried. I raged. I clutched at the smallest straws. A bit of movement in two of my toes became, to me, a sign that life would soon return to my legs. When this small hope faded, I dropped deeper into depression and anger.

Others — Grandpapa, Cal, and Uncle Horace especially — tried to talk with me about my physical state, but my mind rebelled. They wanted me to accept what was lost, and in the gentlest of ways, they reminded me of all that I had — my youth, my intelligence, my spirit, the love of my family and friends. I remember Uncle Horace talking to me about the need for faith in times of tragedy and how I could turn to God for comfort and help. He told me of God's great, unknowable plan — that there was always a purpose behind suffering — and he recounted to me the story of his own coming to faith. (I had never before heard about Cousin Elsie's nearly fatal illness when she was a child.) But I angrily dismissed the idea of a Heavenly Father who could love me and yet allow so terrible a fate to befall me. And nothing could break through my grief.

I think that I might have recovered my senses more quickly had Mamma not been such a willing accomplice.

She tried to be kind — I see that now — but her attitude was much the same as mine. She could not accept that I would be crippled for life, that her daughter would be a useless dependent, unable ever to make the brilliant marriage that was her fondest wish. I believe that she resented my condition even more than I did, and she blamed me for making her own life so much more difficult. Her bitterness only inflamed mine. If my own mother had written me off as a broken, worthless thing, how could I think better of myself? And so we both — Mamma and I — sank into our separate seas of self-pity and darkness.

It took another tragic accident to begin my real recovery. It was about a year after my fall. One crisp fall afternoon, Grandpapa decided to take the buggy out for a ride to Tinegrove — home of my Aunt Lora Howard and her family — and asked Mamma and me to accompany him. I really wanted to go, for I enjoyed my occasional breaks from the confinement of my room. But Mamma quickly rejected the notion. It would take too much time, she said, to dress me, and there was no need to delay Grandpapa. I was so used to Mamma's curt ways that I made no protest. I simply stored the moment away in my collection of resentments. How could I have guessed that Mamma's imperious decision may have saved my life that day?

We have never discovered the exact cause of the accident, but they were some miles from Roselands when the horse became frightened and bolted, and Grandpapa lost the reins. The buggy turned over, and Grandpapa fell under one of the wheels. Mamma was thrown out into a ditch by the roadside. It was Mr. Leland of Fairview and one of his men who came upon the scene soon after and brought Mamma and Grandpapa back to Roselands. Both were unconscious, though Mamma, at first appearance, had suffered little more than a cut to her head.

Dr. Barton was summoned immediately, and a servant went to fetch Uncle Horace from The Oaks. As Grandpapa's injuries seemed more serious, Dr. Barton went to him first. Trapped in my room, all I knew of what was occurring was gleaned from the shouts of the servants in the driveway and the snatches of conversation I overheard as people hurried up and down the hall outside my door. I was seized with fear. Mamma and Grandpapa — could they be dead? Oh, why had I not been kinder to Mamma? Why had I not been able to kiss Grandpapa before he left that day? And selfishly I thought, what will I do without them? Who will care for me?

It was a long time after I heard Dr. Barton arrive that Dick came to my room. He was pale and unsmiling when he entered, and I imagined the worst. But seeing my anxiety, Dick quickly said, "They are alive, dear Sister. Grandpapa has been badly hurt. He has a broken leg and broken arm and many cuts and bruises. But he's a remarkable old fellow, Molly, and the doctor says that with good care he should recover. He came to consciousness soon after he was brought in, and in spite of his pain, he began giving orders to us all."

"Oh, thank God," came from my lips without my bidding. And I asked of Mamma.

"She is still unconscious," Dick said, sitting in the chair beside mine. "She lies upon her bed, and except for a small cut and swelling upon her forehead, she appears merely asleep. But the doctor says that she may have suffered a hard blow, and he cannot ascertain the extent of the damage until she wakens."

"When will that be?" I asked with a growing sense of dread.

"Dr. Barton cannot say," Dick replied. "Perhaps in hours, perhaps in days."

"Or never?"

"That is a possibility," my brother replied, lowering his head.

My old resentment rose, but not for myself. "If only I could walk!" I cried. "If I were not virtually chained to this chair, I could go to her and nurse her! Oh, Dick, all my anger at her seems so petty now. How I wish I could take back every mean word and thought I ever had for her."

"I know," he said softly, taking my hands. "I have all the same regrets, and more. I have never made her life easy with my pranks and thoughtlessness. Yet I love her, Sister, I really do. Let's pray for her. Just you and I together."

He took my hands in his, and he began to pray. He wasn't very good at it; his words came out in a jumble that would have made little sense to anyone save me. But I knew he was begging for our mother's life. I could not bring myself to join in, for I had no faith in a power beyond this world. But when Dick finished speaking with a small sob, I said "Amen" and hugged him as best I could. At that moment, I believed that we were soon to become orphans.

From Molly's journal, dated September 22, 1874:

No, we did not lose our mother. But we did not regain her either.

Mamma remained unconscious for more than a week, and her awakening, when it came, was slow and painful. Dick brought reports to me almost every hour. Mamma had opened her eyes . . . . She had spoken but her words were unintelligible . . . . Mamma was babbling now, as if she were a child. She was asking for her own mother . . . . Mamma had fallen asleep at last, curled up like a baby and sucking her thumb . . . . Mamma had waked and demanded honey and bread and her doll . . . .

With each new report, my worries grew. Surely this was not normal, I thought. But it was several days before Dr. Barton made his final diagnosis. He had sent Dick to sit with me in my room, and soon after, the doctor and Uncle Horace (who had been devoting himself night and day to watching over Grandpapa) entered.

Dr. Barton was both kindly and straightforward when he told us the news. Our mother's brain had been damaged by the blow to her head, and she had reverted to the mental state of a child. Her memory of her life past the age of five or six seemed wholly gone, and bar some miracle, she would need constant attention for the rest of her life. The doctor said that she could be retaught some basic skills, but the process would be long and require a skilled teacher. There was little, he added, that Dick or I could do except to show her great kindness and patience and to pray for her.

Somehow, the doctor's words did not surprise me or Dick, but what Uncle Horace said next shocked us deeply. Because Grandpapa would need close care for some months until his leg and arm fully healed, Aunt Louise's time would be greatly limited, for she was to be Grandpapa's chief nurse and caretaker. Cal would take over the management of the plantation. And Mamma could no longer be available for us. It had been decided that Bob and Betty were to move to The Oaks and that Dick and I would live at Ion with Cousin Elsie and Mr. Travilla.

Dick jumped up and demanded, "For how long?" I looked at him and saw his face redden with embarrassment. He quickly added, "We are very grateful, Uncle Horace. I only meant that it will be hard to separate our family for a long time."

Uncle Horace came forward and put an arm around Dick's shoulders.

"I hope it will not be a lasting separation," he said gently. "And given the proximity of The Oaks and Ion, I believe you will see your stepbrother and stepsister almost as often as you do now. Your Cousin Elsie wanted to take all four of you into her home, but I am convinced that is too much for her to manage right now. At The Oaks, Bob and Betty can continue their studies with me, for you know how I enjoy teaching, and both Aunt Rose and Cousin Rosie are delighted about having young children in the house again. Elsie is looking forward to having you two especially, and I know that you will prosper under her and Edward's wings. I also believe you and Molly can be of great help to Elsie while you are at Ion."

I could see that, having absorbed this announcement, Dick was reacting with favor. My feelings, however, were less felicitous.

"How can I help Cousin Elsie?" I asked, unable to mask the bitterness in my voice. "We are poor relations, but at least Dick is strong and healthy. I am just a useless cripple and will make a bothersome guest. I can help no one, and Cousin Elsie does not need the added burden of looking after me."

Horace came to sit down beside me. He looked into my face. I could see his weariness, and his countenance was stern, but there was tenderness in his eyes as he said, "Elsie asked for you specifically. She and Edward have always loved you, and she does not think of you as a burden."

"But neither can I help her," I declared. "No more than I can help myself."

"You have lost the use of your legs, Molly," Uncle Horace said firmly, "but not your mind or your heart. You are too young and too smart to give in to self-pity."

I tried to protest, but Uncle Horace would not listen. He went on. "You have to trust me. Elsie does need your help, and whether you can walk or not has no meaning for her. Elsie sees *you*, dear girl, not your condition. And I believe that you can assist and support one another right now."

"But what can I do for her, Uncle?" I pleaded. "I have so little to offer."

"You are thinking in material terms," he told me. "It's true you have no money or goods to bestow. But those things are meaningless to Elsie and Edward. I cannot give you an exact answer, but I know you can do a great deal for others if you are willing to open that heart of yours."

There was no more I could say, but Uncle Horace had given me much to ponder. For more than a year, I had thought of myself as only helpless and pitiful. Was it possible that I could have purpose? Could I be of value to someone like my beautiful, wealthy cousin and her generous husband? Everything I had believed to that moment told me that Uncle Horace was mistaken. But something about the way he spoke with such confidence gave me the first glimmer of real hope I had experienced since my dark journey began. I raised no more objections. Fearfully, I accepted the decision of my elders because I had no other choice. But that faint, faint glimmer of hope — somehow it beckoned me forward to life at Ion.

CHAPTER

2

Molly's Story Continues

Jesus said, "Let the little children come to me . . ."

MATTHEW 19:14

Molly's Story Continues

From Molly's journal, dated September 23, 1874:

Our welcome at Ion was every bit as gracious as Uncle Horace had predicted. Cousin Elsie had allotted a room for me on the ground floor near the rear of the house. So defensive was I about my crippled condition that I suspected she had selected this location to keep me out of sight. But when Mr. Travilla carried me into the room, I instantly regretted my dark thoughts. My new "home" was large and airy — the walls a pale, warm yellow. White lace curtains fluttered at the windows, and a tall, wide doorway opened from the room unto a small, stone-paved porch that overlooked the garden. The room was beautifully furnished, and there were bouquets of golden fall blossoms in vases on the low chest of drawers and the bedside table. As I scanned the room, my eye quickly traveled to a colorful quilt that lay folded upon the bed. When I commented upon the beauty of the quilt, Cousin Elsie explained that it was the work of Mr. Travilla's mother. Then I noticed a desk placed beneath one of the windows and the odd-looking chair that sat beside it. At first I thought the chair to be a jarring element, but then I saw that it was the perfect choice — a wheeled chair of the latest design.

Tears swam in my eyes as Mr. Travilla carried me across the room and lowered me gently into the chair. I touched the wheels gingerly as if they were made of the most precious gold.

19

"Is it comfortable?" Cousin Elsie asked. I could only nod and smile in reply, for my voice seemed caught in my throat.

"We are assured," Cousin Elsie continued, "that with practice you can learn to maneuver it yourself, although you may not have the chance. Ever since we unpacked the chair, Harold and Herbert have been arguing over who shall be your 'driver.'"

"Oh, Cousin Elsie and Mr. Travilla," I managed at last. "It is all so wonderful. So much more than I . . . than I ever . . . "

"Whatever you expected, it is no more than you deserve," Cousin Elsie said. "We are just so very grateful that you and Dick have agreed to stay with us."

"And from this moment forward," Mr. Travilla added with that famous twinkle of his, "I claim the right of kin by marriage. You and Dick must address me as 'Cousin Edward,' for we shall be as dear to one another as true cousins."

Dick's room was next to mine and just as beautiful, though masculine in design and exactly to his taste. Placing us on the ground level of the house, Elsie said, was for our convenience (she meant, for my own) and so that I could join in all the family's activities with ease. There seemed to be no detail that Cousin Elsie and Cousin Edward had overlooked. I was thrilled to learn that I would join Missy and Violet in their classroom — a joy for me since Mamma had always regarded academic pursuits as needless distractions for young ladies.

Dick, too, was to continue his studies, attending the local boys' academy in which Eddie was enrolled.

That first day at Ion, all my doubts about our position there were banished forever. The welcome we received from the Travilla children was no less open and generous than that of their parents. I knew my young cousins, of course, but I soon learned how very little I really knew about them. To me, the Travillas had been the "rich relatives" whom my mother and my Aunt Louise envied so openly. Before my accident, I had loved to go to Ion when we were invited because the house was so beautiful and the food always so wonderful. But infected with Mamma's attitude, I had regarded the Travillas themselves as snobs.

I made a promise to be truthful in this journal, so I must admit that I was the true snob. I looked down on my Travilla cousins from my pride. And I assumed that Dick and I were the superior ones because we had so much less and because they were spoiled in every way by their wealth and privileges. Oh, how wrong I was! My cousins, I realized, have no false sense of themselves. They are completely natural in their ways and have always regarded me as their equal. Like their parents, the young Travillas are deeply committed to their faith and look upon their privileges with humility. I was reared to regard religion as unimportant and church as just another social event, so I found the Travillas' practices strange and unsettling at first. I decided, however, to accept their odd religious habits as simply a difference that I could live with. But I shall return to that subject later.

Elsie's Great Hope

As we settled into our new life at Ion, I began to see what interesting people my cousins are. And they have grown dearer to me with each passing day. The children became individuals to me, distinct in their interests and personalities. Missy, the closest to my own age, is a quiet and thoughtful girl, and nearly a duplicate of her beautiful mother in appearance and manner. Violet — who was just six when I moved to Ion — is nearly the exact opposite in temperament, spirited and emotional and given to hasty actions at times. How clearly I can remember her then, the bright-eyed little fairy, her curls bobbing, who would dash into my room each morning before breakfast and plant a quick kiss upon my cheek. At eleven now, she is less inclined to run into my room but still comes to me each day, like sunshine, for her kiss.

Eddie has Vi's emotional bent, though he struggles mightily to control his instinct to act before he thinks. He has the dark hair and handsome features of his father, and at fifteen, he shows signs of reaching his father's full height. Eddie can be mischievous, but it is the twins, Harold and Herbert, who are the inheritors of their father's sense of humor. They are nine now, and in appearance as alike as two peas in a pod.

Then there is Lily, who was born not long after the terrible trouble with the Ku Klux Klan. She was just a year old when Dick and I came to live at Ion, and I must admit that I paid little attention to her at first. In part that is because I was unaccustomed to babies, but also because Lily was often ill and absent from family gatherings. I did not know what was wrong and did not ask, but I concluded from things said that Lily was born with a weakness in her heart. Even I could see that she was frail, but there was something else about her that I could not explain. People often call babies "angels," but for no other infant was this description so apt.

Two more little Travillas have arrived since I came to Ion: Rosemary, a lovely little charmer born in 1870, and baby Daniel, whom we all call "Danny," born in this year of 1874.

Of the rest of the residents of Ion, I shall give a few brief descriptions, for they all play their parts in my story. There are Mr. and Mrs. Daly and their two young sons. The Travillas had met the Daly family during a trip to Viamede, which is Cousin Elsie's plantation in Louisiana. Mr. Daly was teaching at a school there, but because his health is somewhat fragile, he apparently expressed his desire to return to a cooler climate at some time. Then when Lily was born, Cousin Elsie and Cousin Edward found themselves so occupied with the care of their sweet baby that teaching the other children (as the parents had always done) was increasingly difficult. And so Cousin Edward wrote to Mr. Daly, offering him the position of tutor at Ion and asking if Mrs. Daly would consider becoming the head housekeeper as well. Both offers were accepted, and the Dalys were able to come to Ion within a month. I can state from my experience that Mr. Daly is a strict but inspiring teacher, and Mrs. Daly is a kind companion and highly competent manager of this large house and its people.

Of all the servants and employees, I must admit my special fondness for Aunt Chloe and her husband, Joe. Elderly now, Aunt Chloe has been with Cousin Elsie for all her life and is still her most devoted guardian. Joe, whom I guess to be well past eighty, is as lively in mind and spirit as a twenty-year-old man, despite his arthritis. He is also a master of plainspoken common sense. Their granddaughter, Dinah, also lives on the estate with her husband and children. She is the mistress of the school for the children of the servants — a woman of remarkable grace and intelligence.

But what of my other family? What has become of them in the nearly five years since I came to Ion? Bob and Betty were welcomed into Uncle Horace's family with all the love that Dick and I received here at Ion. Under the care of Aunt Rose and the tutelage of Uncle Horace, I have seen them both grow strong and self-confident. I do believe that the presence of children at The Oaks works as a tonic upon Uncle Horace, for despite his gray hair, he seems but a boy at times.

Dear Dick — the best brother a girl could ever wish for — is away from us now. He is living in Philadelphia with the Allisons, Aunt Rose's parents, and is in his second year of medical study. His interest in medicine is a kind of gift for our mother, for I believe that in his heart, Dick hopes some day to find a cure for her. When I made that point to him once, he laughed at first. Then he said that he might never be able to cure Mamma, but that he wanted the opportunity to help her and others. He took my hand and looked deep into my eyes. Then he said that miracles were the province of God, but that God had given us minds capable of understanding many things. To become a doctor, Dick said, meant learning how to heal when possible but also to relieve suffering and to comfort those in pain and sorrow.

Mamma is not in pain. She remains in the world of child-hood to which she awoke after her accident. Cousin Elsie has provided full-time nurses at Roselands because Mamma, like any child of six, must be constantly supervised lest she harm herself. She is very willful and thoughtless of others, but strangely gay and imaginative. Her closest companion is a doll she had as a child, and she treats it as sweetly as any mother ever treated her babe. She does not remember Dick or me; to her, we are only playmates who visit on occasion. I do not pity my mother for she does not know that she suffers, and I no longer feel any anger toward her. But I sometimes wonder if she was as loving with Dick and me when we were small as she is now with that doll. I think perhaps she was — that she always loved us in her way.

Grandpapa did recover, but his injuries and his age have hobbled him. Aunt Louise is his mainstay. She seems less cold with him than with the rest of us, but her haughtiness has by no means disappeared. A bit of good fortune came her way several years ago; her sister-in-law, a wealthy and childless matron named Mrs. Delaford, took on the responsibility of educating Isadora and Virginia. It seems that Mrs. Delaford is considering leaving her money to my cousins, so long as Isa and Virgy dance to her tune. Mrs. Delaford sent both Isa and Virgy to an expensive finishing school in the North. But my cousins have completed their education, and now they are "husband-hunting" in a manner that makes Isa, at least, deeply uncomfortable. But Aunt Louise and Virgy are willing puppets, so Isa must go along, I suppose.

Cal is running Roselands with great skill, and Wally Conley has just entered West Point. Grandpa is so proud of them. And there is another doctor in the family! Arthur Conley — my bookish, serious cousin — completed his medical studies and has recently returned to his home here to begin practice with Dr. Barton. I see him often now and with great pleasure. He tends to little Lily, and he usually stops in to chat with me when he visits. He is a dedicated reader, and he has been most encouraging of my decision to become a writer. Arthur is like Dick, too, in his dedication to others, and his visits lessen my sadness that Dick is away for so long . . . .

From Molly's journal, dated October 2, 1874:

I have never known Ion to be so silent. The servants walk about on tiptoe, and everyone speaks in whispers. I haven't seen Cousin Elsie or Cousin Edward for days. I join Missy and the others in the dining room for meals, but none of us has any appetite for food. I do what I can to help. Rosemary often comes to my room to play, and her happiness lightens my very soul while she is with me. Yet her round little face, sturdy body, and sparkling laughter are also reminders of the sorrow in this house, for Rosemary's good health is so starkly in contrast with that of our little angel, Lily.

When I began this journal, we all were extremely hopeful that Lily's condition was improving. Cousin Elsie and Cousin Edward had, upon the advice of a noted heart specialist, taken Lily north to a health resort for the summer. Their letters indicated that Lily was gaining strength and seemed to be benefiting from the clean, mountain air of the resort and the elixirs prescribed by the physician. Then a week ago, a letter arrived telling us that the Travillas were returning. Lily had taken a turn for the worse, and since the weather here is cooling now, they wanted to bring her home to her family. They arrived two days after their letter, and Lily is now unable to leave her bed.

Cousin Elsie and then Cousin Edward came to see me after their return. Each parent spoke of hope for their child's life, but I knew that they are terribly distressed. Cousin Elsie is more thin and pale than I have ever seen her, and Cousin Edward — always so full of life and jokes — appears bent beneath the burden of his woe. His visit with me was brief, and as I said, he talked of hope. Yet just before he left my room, he requested two things of me. He asked if I would be able to help with the younger children should they need attention. (I assured him that I would.) And then he asked for my prayers — for Lily's recovery if that is God's will, and if it is not, for her eternal rest in the loving arms of our Lord. And I have prayed almost without cease. I have not the ability to get down upon my knees, but I know our Heavenly Friend hears me nevertheless.

If this journal were intended for readers other than myself, they might well wonder what brought me, the girl who had no faith, to this state. Is it not passing strange that I, Molly Percival, who could only rant and rage at her own misfortune, should now turn to prayer in the face of this far more devastating tragedy?

I owe my faith to my Lord, but it was Cousin Elsie who directed me upon His path. My conversion was no easy or sudden thing. Nor did my cousin hound me to accept her beliefs. She told me once that the Dinsmore blood flowing in our veins is a source of great strength but also of a stubbornness that can be slow to change. She knew better, she said, than to try compelling me to share her faith.

When I came here, I understood that Ion is a Christian home. But I really had no idea what that meant. I rather expected an excess of piety and constant Bible-reading. What I found were not self-righteous displays of religion, but people who live their faith in every way. From the youngest to the eldest member of this household, employers and employees alike, the people of Ion are unfailingly kind to one another and thoughtful of needs not their own. The jealousies and envy that were so much a part of life with Mamma and Aunt Louise were simply not present at Ion. For the first time in my life, I found myself among people who did not indulge in gossip and backbiting. There was no discussion of who is better or prettier or has more than someone else.

Not that all is perfection. The Travilla children have quarrels like all children and are often corrected for this and that behavior. But the tone of the correction is so different from my own experience. Cousin Elsie and Cousin Edward teach their children with the most compassionate balance of gentleness and firmness. The parents do not simply command obedience; they explain why their rules are important. And the children comply because they understand what is expected of them. Punishments, when required, are fair and intended to teach, not to hurt. The respect that the parents have for their children is reflected back in the respect of each young Travilla for the parents and for each other.

I once asked Cousin Elsie about her principles for rearing children, and she quoted from a letter written by the apostle Paul to Titus: "Similarly, encourage the young men to be self-controlled. In everything set them an example by doing what is good. In your teaching show integrity, seriousness and soundness of speech that cannot be condemned . . . . " Jesus, she said, set the example for parents by loving all His children without reserve but also expecting love and obedience in return. By loving Him and following His commands and precepts, Christians are preparing for eternal life. That is the model, Elsie said, for parents to follow in teaching their children and preparing them for life in this world as responsible and loving adults. Parents must set the standards and *live up to them*, she emphasized.

But can a parent forgive a child who does something truly bad, I wondered. Yes, of course, Elsie assured me, for parents love a child's heart and because of that love, they can forgive the behavior. But they cannot overlook or tolerate it. Parents, she said, have the duty to show children the difference between right and wrong and to teach that we must ask for forgiveness and do our best to make right whatever we have done wrong. As we adjusted to life at Ion, Dick and I both had many such conversations with my dear cousin. And not once did Cousin Elsie preach at us or tell us what we must think and believe.

I had many bad times during my first year or so at Ion. I tried to accept my paralysis, but the cruelest part of my fate was knowing what I had lost. I knew what it was to walk and run and dance. I knew what it was to rise from my bed in the morning and walk to my dressing table. I knew the feel of grass beneath my bare feet and skipping across the lawn when the dew is still fresh. I knew the pinpricks of cold that gripped my toes when I played in snow. I knew the soft touch of cotton on my legs when I wriggled into clean stockings. And now I would never feel any of those sensations again. I tried to hold my anger and resentment inside, but the emotions were too strong and would burst forth.

There came a day when, frustrated because I had dropped a book upon the floor and could not retrieve it without calling for help, I broke down in tears and wept as I had never wept before. Aunt Chloe found me thus and called for Cousin Elsie. She came into my room, sat beside me on the bed, and cradled me in her arms. But she said nothing. She only held me close until at last the storm of tears subsided. Then she bathed my face with a cool cloth and said, "You are very afraid, aren't you, Molly?"

I was startled. I knew myself to be angry and bitter and self-indulgent and unable to control my feelings — all qualities that I hated in myself and blamed on my crippled condition. But I had never thought myself afraid. Without hesitating, however, I replied, "How did you know?"

Cousin Elsie continued to wipe my face and spoke in gentle tones. "Fear is as natural to humans as love and laughter. It can grip us and then disappear in an instant. But it can also burrow down inside us and affect everything we feel and think and do. I see it in you because I have felt it myself. No, I will not pretend that I understand your suffering, dear Molly, for I have only once experienced the kind of physical pain you endured and it ended with my recovery. But I have known fear of failing those I love and fear of never being loved. I was about your age when fear of admitting I was wrong in my judgment of another brought me to the brink of making a mistake that would have ruined my life. I know what it is like to feel angry and helpless, but underneath those feelings, fear is the most harmful, I think."

"I am afraid, Cousin Elsie," I admitted slowly as soft tears came to my eyes, "so terribly afraid. I'm afraid of the future. How will I live as half a person? What is life for me when I cannot walk through it? Who will care for me? I am now but a burden to myself and everyone around me. Oh, Cousin Elsie, I'm afraid to die and just as fearful of living on like this."

"But you did not die, and for that, we all thank God. So you must live. I believe with all my heart that God saved you for a purpose. But it is your choice whether to discover that purpose and find the path that God has planned for you or to let your fear of living overwhelm you and keep you in darkness."

"What purpose could God have for me?" I asked.

"I do not know," Cousin Elsie said plainly. "God alone knows, and the way to learn His purpose is to open your heart to Him and listen to Him. It may not be easy, for you must confront your fears. I wish I could do it for you,

Molly, but that is beyond our human abilities. But there is One who will be your guide and protector—our Lord Jesus Christ."

"Why would He care about a useless, pointless thing like me?" I responded with a trace of my old anger.

"Because He loves you and because He alone knows all that you suffer," Cousin Elsie said, hugging me close again. "He died for you and me and for all humankind. Think, Molly. Do you believe He would have made that sacrifice if not from love? He gave His life for us when He was a man, and then He rose from death so that He might give us help and hope and eternal love. You have but to invite Him into your heart to know the peace He offers."

"How?" I beseeched. "How do I open my heart when I do not even know how to pray?"

"Prayer is but a conversation from the heart with your best Friend," she answered, raising my face gently and warming me with her smile. "And I know you can converse. Remember that so long as your words are true, He listens and answers. May I offer a prayer with you now? I would like to ask Our Lord for His blessings upon you as you begin your journey to Him."

"Yes, please," I said gratefully. I closed my eyes and bowed my head and listened to her words. There was nothing elaborate in what she said. Her prayer was simple and brief and straight from her heart. When she finished, we continued to sit together for some time. She held me but said no more. I'm sure she understood that my mind was racing. That I might have some purpose in this world? It was a wondrous thought.

I must have fallen asleep in Cousin Elsie's arms, but she was gone when I awoke. She had left me something, though. A small Bible with a ribbon marking a place in the book of Matthew lay upon my quilt. A small note was there, too, in Cousin's clear handwriting: "Chapters 27 and 28 will tell you of our Lord's great suffering and the promise He brings us all. I will be most happy to discuss more with you, as you like." She had signed the note simply with a swirling E.

I read the chapters and I wept softly for the fate of Jesus. The pain He felt and the heartbreaking moment when He questioned the purpose of His suffering. Yes, I thought, Jesus would understand my feelings. He, too, had felt pain and loss and grief. Then, having read of His death and resurrection, I turned to the beginning of Matthew and read of Jesus' life. I had heard the stories often before, in church, but never before did I take in their meaning.

As I have written, mine was not a miraculous conversion. But from that day, I was a willing student with the Holy Bible as my text. Cousin Elsie and Cousin Edward were always available to me to discuss, answer questions, and yes, to argue all the points that confused or troubled me. Gradually, I began to understand that the book was not a collection of stories, but my map for the road I wanted to travel. As my fear left me, my anger and hostility and resentment fled as well. My heart, freed of its dark fears and pain, opened, and I was reborn.

Elsie's Great Hope

From Molly's journal, dated October 7, 1874:

Arthur has just left me. He and Dr. Barton are both attending Lily. She is awake, he says, yet her strength is all but gone, and there is nothing left for any doctor to do. Elsie and Edward and Uncle Horace and Aunt Rose are with her. And Missy, Eddie, and Vi. It is nearly midnight, and Arthur says that he doubts our little angel will see the dawn. That hope has flown, but a greater hope sustains us all, that we shall be reunited again someday in the love of our Father and Friend. Oh, dear God, cherish the precious, pure soul of our Lily and . . .

CHAPTER

3

Sadness and Joy

My eyes have grown dim with grief; my whole frame is but a shadow.

JOB 17:7

*H*orace Dinsmore led his elder daughter to the couch near the fireplace in the library. When she was seated, he picked up a knitted shawl that lay on the couch and spread it around her shoulders. Then he turned and took a poker and jabbed at the logs in the fire, making the flames leap. He held his hands near the heat. At last, he sat down beside Elsie. Taking her cold hands in his own warm ones, he rubbed gently.

"It is a surprisingly chilly day for early October," he said.

"Yes, Papa, but clear and bright nonetheless," she replied. Her voice, he was glad to hear, was even. He was very worried about her. The previous months had taken their toll; Elsie was very pale, and she had lost weight so that her face was drawn. Dark half-moons under her beautiful eyes added to the thin appearance, and her hands in his seemed to have no weight at all.

"I must go to our visitors, Papa," she said, but she made no effort to rise. "I had not expected so many to be with us today."

"Sit for a while, my dear," he said. "Your mother is handling everything. She and Mrs. Daly and Crystal will see that your visitors are made comfortable, and Edward is with the children. You may go to them when you are warmed."

"And Molly?"

"Aunt Chloe is keeping an eye on her."

"It was a fine service, wasn't it, Papa?" Elsie asked in a flat tone. She sank back against the pillows of the couch and seemed to become even smaller.

"Yes, Daughter, it was. Reverend Wood spoke eloquently, and the readings were particularly fitting."

"I'm glad you think so, Papa. Edward and I chose the verses that Lily — that Lily loved best."

On saying her daughter's name, Elsie's voice had faltered, and Horace felt the small tremor that passed through her body. She took a deep breath and then continued, saying, "I feel such an emptiness inside myself, Papa. I know that our loving Father has released my child from her pain and suffering and that she is with Him and Mamma in Heaven. I know that she is now whole and healthy and bathed in His love. Believe me, Papa, I know that Lily is happy. But I feel as if a part of me has been ripped away."

Elsie lowered her head to hide her tears, but Horace could hear the pain in her voice as she went on. "This grief, Papa," she said. "It is more powerful than I had thought possible, and I fear it will overwhelm me. I should be joyful, Papa, that Lily has reached the destination to which we all aspire, and I am. But still I want her here with me, in my arms, that I might hold her and comfort her and tell her of my love."

Suddenly, her head snapped up, and she stared into her father's face. "How selfish I am to feel this way!" she exclaimed. "Is my faith so weak that I can only dwell upon my loss? Oh, Papa, I feel that I might die from this sadness!"

Horace moved one hand away from hers and reached his arm around her shoulders, drawing her close.

"Grief is not a betrayal of faith," he said. "Do you remember what Jesus told His disciples? 'Now is your time of grief, but I will see you again and you will rejoice, and no one will take away your joy.' Jesus knew that His disciples would mourn Him, yet He did not belittle their grief. Why, Jesus Himself wept with grief at the tomb of Lazarus, before restoring the brother of Mary and Martha to life. Remember, too, these words from Ecclesiastes, that there is a season for everything — 'a time to weep and a time to laugh, a time to mourn and a time to dance . . . .'

"The emptiness you feel, my beloved Elsie, is not selfish. You are a mother. You carried your child inside you and gave birth to her. She was of your flesh and now that part of you has gone on. Would you begrudge the sorrow of a man who has lost a leg or an eye? I know that you wouldn't. Nor can you judge yourself harshly for your own sorrow. All the feelings we have are given us by God, and He has given us the capacity for grief as well as joy. Think of this from the book of Lamentations: 'Though He brings grief, He will show compassion, so great is His unfailing love.' He knows that we must suffer and mourn, but He is the light that will guide us out of our darkness."

Then Horace asked, "Does your grief shake your faith?"

Elsie looked up again in surprise. "Oh, no, Papa," she said with passion. "Nothing can do that. I know in the deepest part of my heart that God has taken Lily to serve His purpose and that my child is with Him, as we all hope to be one day."

"Then do not doubt yourself, my dearest," Horace replied softly. "The emptiness will heal, but you must give it time. Lily will always be a part of you, and when your sorrow has run its course, you will feel the fullness of your joy for her. I know that to be true. Your own mother is still a part of me though she has been gone for forty years. My happiness for her has long since banished the feelings of anger and grief that overwhelmed me when I learned of her death."

Horace took a handkerchief from his pocket and put it into Elsie's hand. "I will not admonish you, as I so often did when you were a child, to stop your tears," he said. "I have learned that crying is not a sign of weakness but a sweet release from pain. Yet I am your father, and I claim the right to express my concern for your health and well-being. Mourn, my child, because you must. We must all mourn our loss this day and for many days to come. But do not forget those whom God has left in your care. They need your strength, and they need to share in your grieving. None of you will be the better for trying to bear this sadness alone."

"Thank you, Papa," Elsie said, dabbing at her eyes, "for the handkerchief and for hearing my worries. You reminded me of my own duties to my beloved family. And you are right that grief is easier to bear when it is shared."

"Then turn to your Heavenly Friend for guidance and consolation as you always have. Open your heart to Him, and He will comfort you. With His help, you and Edward will comfort your children."

"I will go to them," Elsie said, "but may we remain here a few minutes more? Though I am a mother, I am still your child, and I need your support. It feels right to rest upon your shoulder for a bit."

She laid her head against her father's shoulder, and he stroked her hair as he had done so many times when she was a girl. Long ago, Horace had tried to barricade himself from all sadness behind a wall of arrogance and pride. How far he had come in his understanding. As he sheltered Elsie in his arms, he lifted a silent prayer: *Dear God, please help my child through her sorrow. And help me to be Your obedient servant. I am as nothing without You, Lord. I need Your strength to be strong for Elsie and her family. Please help me, Father, that I may help others. Amen.*

"I am glad Elsie was able to speak with so many of the mourners today," Rose was saying to Edward about an hour later. Elsie had just gone to tend to baby Danny, and Horace and Rosie were in the parlor, talking with the other children. Rose and Edward were standing together in the hallway where they had bid farewell to the last of the visitors.

"Yes, I think it has done her some good to know how widely loved Lily is," Edward replied. Then he added. "I suppose I should say how loved she *was*, but that seems wrong. The love is still here, though Lily has left us."

"Lily will always be with us," Rose said, putting her hand on Edward's arm. "I learned so much from that child in the short while she was here. So much about courage and humility and the true meaning of hope and love."

A small smile came to Edward's lips. "She was a remarkable child," he said. "Every day with her was something precious, a gift of love from God."

"We will all miss her dreadfully," Rose whispered.

"Yes, we will, but shall I tell you something strange? I do not feel as if I have lost her. She is here" — he laid his hand to his breast — "in my heart, and she always will be. She is with our Father in Heaven, yet she is also here with me. I feel as if my heart were enlarged by her presence just as each of my children makes me grow and strive to be better. My sorrow is that I shall not see her again until we are reunited in Heaven. I shall always wonder what her life may have been had she lived. But, Rose, my little girl accomplished a great deal among us. She gave love to so many."

Rose, too, smiled as she said, "I will never forget her last words — 'Jesus loves me.'"

"She wanted us to know that He was there for her, ready to take her hand and lead her on," Edward added. "I believe

that. And I believe her last thought was to comfort us. I want the other children to understand that."

"They need you now, Edward. The young ones, of course, but Missy, Eddie, and Molly as well. And Vi — I am somewhat worried about her. I tried to talk with her, but each time I said Lily's name, Vi hurriedly changed the subject."

"I have also noticed her reaction," Edward said, his expression now solemn. "There has been so little time these past few days, but I will speak privately with her today."

"Do that, Edward, for I fear she is trying to disguise her feelings. She does not cry, and she barely speaks. That is not like our openhearted Vi. But she will talk to you. She adores her Papa, you know."

"Then let us join the others now, and I will find the appropriate moment to get her aside."

Edward did find his moment. He and Rose had been talking with the others for some quarter of an hour when he saw Violet silently moving away from the group. In an instant, she slipped from the room. Edward felt certain he knew where she was going, so he delayed a few minutes before taking his leave from the rest of his family.

When she was about five, Vi had discovered a corner of a luggage room on the second floor where trunks, valises, and boxes had been stacked in such a way as to create a small cubicle. This space, hidden from sight, became her secret hideaway, and she would retreat to it when she wanted to be alone. How many games of imagination she had played there. The luggage and boxes had been at one time or another the walls of mighty castles and of elegant ballrooms. The little space had been a shop where Vi sold silks and ribbons to fantasy customers, a schoolroom where she "taught" her dolls to read and write, and many other settings for her creative games. As she grew older, Vi had continued to go to the storage room when she wanted to be alone with her thoughts. She would read or daydream or ponder problems there.

Her parents knew about her secret place and respected it. Elsie and Edward understood that in a large family, children needed times to be solitary. But now Edward decided that he must enter Vi's little world and draw her out.

Opening the door to the room, he said her name softly. "Vi, it is Papa. May I come in?"

Her sweet voice replied, "Yes, Papa."

He crossed the room to the little, boxed-off area in the far corner. Peering over a pile of hatboxes, he saw her sitting on the floor. He saw also that she was holding an old baby doll in her arms.

"May I join you?" he asked.

Vi looked up and replied simply, "Yes, Papa."

Though the space was narrow, there was enough room for Edward to sit down opposite his child, folding his long legs beneath him so that he sat cross-legged just as Vi did. She smiled at his odd posture.

"You have not played with that doll for a long time," he observed.

"She was my favorite doll, Papa, when Lily was born."

"So you remember Lily's birth?"

"Oh, yes, Papa. She was such a pretty baby. And you and Mamma were so worried about her. And now she's gone, and you and Mamma are sad for her."

Edward hesitated. His impulse was to take his darling daughter into his arms and hold her safely to him forever. Instead, he asked, "Are you sad, Vi dear?"

"I think I am, Papa," she answered. "I'm sad that I will never see Lily again and that I don't know why."

"What do you mean?" he asked gently. "You know that Lily has gone to be with Jesus, and someday we will all be with her again."

Her lips quivered, and she lowered her face close to the doll's. Almost in a whisper, she said, "I don't know why Jesus had to take her from us. I don't know why Jesus made her die. You said Jesus loves her, but we don't make someone we love die, do we, Papa?"

She looked up, and Edward's heart nearly broke when she said, "Will Jesus make me die and leave you, Papa?"

"Oh, dear child," he said, and he extended his arms toward her. Vi stood up, and the baby doll rolled away from her. She rushed to her father, crumpling into his lap and burying her face against his chest as he embraced her.

"I do not understand myself," Edward said, rocking her as he spoke, "but that is the way it should be. God has a plan for each of us, Vi. He has numbered our hours in this world, and for some, life here is short. But the life Lily has now is eternal. It will never end. Lily is happy now, for Jesus holds her in His arms just as I am holding you, and His love for her is greater than all the love of all the people who have ever lived and ever will live here on earth. She will never again know pain and never suffer. Did you hear her last words for us? She said 'Jesus loves me.' She wanted us to know that she was going to Him. And she wanted us to know her joy."

"I *am* glad for her, Papa," Vi said softly.

44

"As for you and me, we cannot know when our time on earth will be done," Edward went on. "But I think God has many things for you to do before He takes you home. He has given me fifty-six years so far. Is that not a very long time?"

Vi looked up and said, "Very long, Papa. Very long indeed."

Edward could not help himself. He laughed and hugged his daughter close. Then he said, "Very long, and I hope to have longer, if that is God's will. And you may have even more years than I. But however many years we have, God wants us to make the best of our lives. If we think only of the moment of our dying, we will waste the precious time He allots to us. Think of Lily. She was so often weak and ill, but think of the happiness she gave to us in her six years. Now she is bringing happiness in Heaven. But do you know that she lives here too?"

"Where, Papa?" Vi asked in surprise.

Edward put his finger to her chest. "Here," he said, "in your heart." Then he moved his finger to her forehead. "And here, in your mind — in all the memories you have of her. Close your eyes and listen carefully, love. Can you hear her voice, her laughter?"

Vi did as he said, and her face showed that she was concentrating intensely. After several moments, she exclaimed, "I can, Papa! I can hear her laughing at me that day that I dressed up in Mamma's gown and pretended to be Cinderella's ugly sister. Lily thought that was so funny."

"That is a memory, and whenever you think that Lily has left you, you can go to your memories and find her there."

"But shouldn't I be sad when I think of her?" Vi asked. "Shouldn't I cry and be sorrowful?"

"You should be what you feel, dearest," he replied. "I think you do feel sorrow, but that doesn't mean you cannot feel happiness as well for your little sister. You can cry, and you can laugh, and you should respect each feeling. Do you remember the time that Lily and Herbert found me napping in my chair in the little garden? And while I slept, they covered me with ribbons and bits of lace from your Mamma's sewing box and flowers from the garden?"

A little giggle escaped Vi.

"And when they were done," Edward went on, "they got all you children together to view their joke. I awoke to find myself surrounded by all your beaming faces. Then Lily patted my hand and said, 'Papa's a birthday cake.' I cannot help but laugh when I think of that time. I must have looked very silly."

He did laugh — a hearty laugh that Vi hadn't heard for many months — and she joined in. She laughed until tears came to her eyes, and then she cried and her little body shook with sobs. Edward hugged her, and his own tears mingled with hers. After some time, Vi's crying eased, and Edward wiped her face with his handkerchief.

Through her sniffles, the little girl said with some wonderment, "I can feel happy and sad at the same time."

"Of course, you can," Edward assured her. "Human feelings are complicated, Vi. We all feel differently, and sometimes our own feelings seem to be in conflict with one another. People often think they know how other people should feel, but that is not possible. Only God can see into our true hearts. That is why you can talk with Him about feelings you cannot explain even to me and your Mamma."

"I can always talk to you, Papa," Vi declared.

"And I want you to, dearest," he said. "I will always do my very best to listen to you and advise you and share your concerns. But God is the Father of us all. He is your first and best Friend, and He understands your deepest thoughts and feelings. Never be afraid or embarrassed to take your troubles and your joys to Him."

Father and daughter talked together for some time until Edward said, "Vi, I must get up now. If I do not rise, I am afraid that my legs will turn to stone and I will never again move from this spot. Then you will have to visit your poor Papa who has taken root in the luggage room."

Vi giggled as Edward lifted her off his lap, and she extended her hands to help him stand. "I'm glad you came to find me, Papa," she said. "I thought nobody knew where I was."

"Ah, I just made a good guess," he said as he stretched first one leg, then the other to recover from the pins-and-needles sensation of sitting so long. "If you had not been here, I would have put Bruno on your trail."

"Do you remember the time, Papa, when Eddie set Lily on Bruno's back, just like he was a pony and not a dog, and . . ."

Edward took his daughter's hand, and they left the little room as she continued her story. An observer might have wondered at their smiling faces on such a sorrowful day. But no mortal observer could have guessed the power of the emotions that father and daughter shared. Together, Edward and Vi had found their own way to honor their beloved daughter and sister and to hold her in their hearts. Over the weeks and months that followed, the rest of the family would come to share the feeling as well. And whenever any of the Travillas spoke of their departed child, it would be with smiles compounded both of sweet memories and of anticipation for their eternal reunion.

CHAPTER

4

Questions and Answers

*For the LORD searches every heart
and understands every motive
behind the thoughts. If you
seek him, he will be
found by you.*

1 CHRONICLES 28:9

The winter months passed quietly that year. At Ion, The Oaks, and Roselands, the absence of the family's "angel" was keenly felt. The traditional customs of mourning were carefully observed, but among the Travillas and the Dinsmores, it was understood that each person should be allowed to grieve in his own way. Truly, the life and the death of little Lily affected everyone differently. Her parents, grandparents, her older brothers and sisters, her Aunt Rosie, Uncle Trip, and Cousin Molly all felt great sorrow mingled with intense joy. They knew that Lily was with her Father in Heaven, yet they could not help missing her little face and gentle presence. Young Rosemary Travilla was confused and not quite certain where Lily had gone, and her parents were very gentle as they explained that Lily now lived with Jesus.

The family's Christian friends and relatives naturally felt deep sadness for the family, but they too rejoiced at the overwhelming happiness of Lily's reunion with her Heavenly Father. Whatever their faith, everyone in the community who knew Elsie and Edward was touched in some way by their loss. And letters of condolence arrived from friends in all parts of the country and as far away as the capitals of Europe.

At Roselands, Virginia Conley had cried fiercely when she was told of Lily's death, but Isa was too deeply shocked for tears, although she knew how ill the child had been. When the reality sank in, Isa also cried — soft, sad tears shed in solitude. Old Mr. Dinsmore said very little, but he seemed to be more frail and bent as if the burden of his sorrow were more than he could carry. Arthur Conley, who had tended little Lily in her final hours, sought solace in his work and in long conversations with his mentor, Dr. Barton. Cal Conley found himself turning to a higher source — the Bible Elsie had given him years before. Only Louise Conley seemed unruffled by the loss. She went about her duties, which included running the household and overseeing the care of her sister Enna, and hardly ever mentioned the sadness at Ion.

"I don't understand Mother at all," Isa said to Cal one evening when they were alone in the library. "She seems to think that Cousin Elsie and Cousin Edward should just get on with their lives as if nothing had happened to them. But what could be worse than losing a child? How can Mamma be so cold-hearted?"

Cal looked up from his reading. "I believe that our mother has buried her capacity for sorrow as deeply within herself as her capacity for joy," he replied gravely. "I will never forget what happened when we received word that our Papa had been killed. Mamma screamed and sobbed, and I remember feeling afraid that she might die from her grief. She locked herself in her bedroom, and for days we didn't see her. I would go to her room, press my ear against the door, and listen to her weeping just to assure myself that she was still alive. Then one day, she came out. And she has never been the same since."

"How do you mean?" asked Isa, whose own memories of that time were vague.

"Well, she was perfectly attired in black, which was appropriate," Cal continued. "But everything about her appearance was stern and hard. Her face bore no signs of her weeping. In fact, her expression gave no signs of any emotion. For a moment, I could not recognize her. It was as though the person who emerged from that room looked like my mother but was not she. It was frightening, dear Sister, to see her like that — so calm and reserved, as if all her human feelings had turned to ice."

"I don't have those memories," Isa said.

"You were very young," Cal noted. "About six, I think. But I wonder if you remember our mother before Papa died."

"Yes, quite well," Isa reflected. "Even now I can clearly recall her laughter when she played with us. She and Papa always loved to play with us, even at our childish games of hide-and-seek."

"She and Papa were as loving parents as any children could want," Cal said with a soft smile. "But Papa's death and the war changed her, Isa. I have pondered this question for a very long time, and I believe that in her grief for Papa, our mother decided the only way to deal with sorrow was not to allow herself to feel pain and grief again. Not for herself or for anyone else. The problem is that closing one's heart to sadness shuts out love as well."

"Do you think she still loves us?" Isa asked in a gruff whisper.

"Oh, yes," Cal answered with firmness. "She loves us all in her way, and you must admit that she has been a faithful guardian to us. She protected us from harm and saw that we were provided for by bringing us here to Roselands. You know how important our education is to her."

A small groan escaped Isa's lips before she said, "How well I know that. I cringe when I think how Mamma plays up to Mrs. Delaford. It's embarrassing."

"Don't be shamed for Mamma," Cal admonished. "She doesn't court and flatter Mrs. Delaford for her personal gain.

It is you and Virginia she cares for. Mrs. Delaford paid the
bills for your finishing school, but it was Mamma and her
dignity that paid the real price. But we stray from the point.
I cannot see into Mamma's heart, but I think I understand
why she seems so cold and unsympathetic to the Travillas.
She's afraid to feel strongly for others because strong emotions might crack the wall of coldness she has built around
herself. If she grieves for the Travillas, there is the danger
that she will open the door to her own grief again."

Isa — who was, like all the Conley children, very bright
— quickly saw the truth in her brother's musings. "Lily's
death might bring back her feelings when Papa died," Isa
said, "and that she cannot bear."

"Not if she must bear it alone," Cal replied. He got up
from his chair, and holding the Bible in his hand, he crossed
the room to take a seat beside Isa on the couch. "If our
mother only knew the comfort contained within the covers
of this book . . . " he said, letting his words trail off.

"I have noticed how much time you spend with that
Bible," Isa commented. "What is it you find there?"

"Answers," Cal replied, "answers to the most important
questions of all. This book is like a guide to all of life's questions. I have studied it for some years now, and I am constantly amazed that whatever I need, I find it here. When
I am troubled or angry or sad, I can turn to this book and
find an endless source of comfort and guidance."

"Are you a Christian, Cal?" Isa asked with a small note
of surprise in her voice.

Her brother did not answer for some moments. His fin-
gers idly stroked the leather cover of the volume in his hand
as he contemplated Isa's query. Then a smile came to his
lips, and he said, "I believe that I am very close, dear Sister.

Very close. I have learned that faith comes to people in many different ways. For some it arrives in a blinding flash. For those like our Cousin Elsie, it is woven into the very threads of life from early childhood. For people like me, the process seems to be long and daunting. I have resisted much of what I have read in this book. But I have discovered that even when I am most stubborn, the Word does not abandon me."

"But it's only a book," Isa protested.

"Not so," Cal disagreed gently. "It is the message of God to His children. I read the Bible when I was a child and thought it merely a collection of quaint and ancient stories. Then came a time when I was very low and thought myself beyond hope. And Cousin Elsie told me to open my heart and allow God's message in. The way has been hard for me. Yet I have persisted. Now when I read, I really listen to what God is saying to me. I shall never understand it all, but I understand more and more."

"Perhaps I should read it again," Isa said.

"Yes, you should. I cannot tell you what to believe, dear Sister, but I think you should be open to the possibilities contained here. Read and study with your heart as well as your mind — that's my advice. Perhaps we can talk together of our readings," Cal suggested.

"I would like that very much," Isa said, for she had always looked up to her eldest brother and was flattered that he would wish to share his studies with her. Then a question struck her, and she asked, "But where should I begin? Should I start with Genesis?"

"If you like," he said, "but the wonder of the Bible is that you may begin at any place and find what you need. I might recommend, however, that you start with the book of

55

Matthew, for I think the story of Christ's life and death and resurrection will have particular meaning to you now."

When Isa went to her room that night, she had to do some searching to find her own copy of the Bible. At last, she uncovered it buried at the bottom of a chest with some old schoolbooks. As she dusted the cover with a handkerchief, she felt an odd sense of regret that she had neglected the book for so many years. Could Cal be right, she wondered as she turned the pages and came to the first chapter of Matthew. Were there answers here to the questions that she had never been able to answer? *There's only one way to know*, she said to herself, *and that is to begin.* So Isa settled into her chair beside the fireplace and read. And the oil lamp that lighted her reading blazed for many hours that night.

Isa's Bible study soon became a kind of passion for her, and she and Cal spent nearly every evening in deep and engrossing conversation. Other members of the household naturally noticed her new interest, and some pointed comments were directed her way. Virginia chided her sister, in a friendly sort of way, for endangering her youthful complexion by spending so much time with an old book. "You'll get wrinkles," Virgy laughed, "and no man wants to marry a girl with wrinkles." Arthur, on the other hand, encouraged Isa's interest and occasionally joined her and Cal in their discussions when he was not making calls on the sick. Always the scholar of the family, Arthur added a perspective that was most enlightening.

Louise also noted Isa's new preoccupation, but she said nothing. It was, she decided, just a passing fancy and would

soon enough fade away. Louise had more pressing worries
for her daughters — namely, how to arrange suitable marriages for them. To Louise, this required finding a supply of
eligible men who could afford to marry girls who possessed
both charm and refinement but no fortunes of their own.
Romance held no attraction for the mother. She had married for love and only suffered heartbreak. No, for Louise,
the purpose of her daughters' marriages would be security,
and any future son-in-law must have wealth or be well on
the road to riches. Her dilemma was how to introduce her
girls into the company of such prospects.

The obvious solution was through the connections of her
sister-in-law, Mrs. Delaford. In truth, Louise did not like
her sister-in-law very much. The woman was overbearing,
opinionated, and openly condescending to her "poor relations." But Mrs. Delaford, who was childless, had taken up
the notion of grooming the Conley girls as she might have
groomed daughters of her own. To that end, she had
insisted that Virginia and Isa attend the boarding school of
her choosing, and she had already taken them, with Louise
along to chaperone, on several holiday visits to various
expensive resorts. In return, Mrs. Delaford expected
absolute obedience to her will. Louise had learned never to
contradict Mrs. Delaford's opinions, no matter how ridicu-
lous, and to play the part of the grateful relative without
complaint. But Louise was a Dinsmore and had inherited
the Dinsmore pride. The more she submitted to Mrs.
Delaford's demands, the greater her resentment.

Virginia had no problem at all following Mrs. Delaford's
desires. Virginia was an intelligent young woman but
cursed with laziness, and her highest ambition was the
same as her mother's — to make a comfortable marriage.

The idea that she might find her own way in the world was appalling to her, and she dismissed the possibility entirely. She would find a wealthy man (who, she assumed, would also be young, handsome, and adoring) and marry him. That she must kowtow to her rich aunt to achieve this goal did not bother her in the least. Mrs. Delaford and her money and social connections were merely the means to an end, and once the dreamed-of marriage was a reality, Virginia was sure that she could free herself of her aunt's control. Not that she was entirely ungrateful; Virginia appreciated that it was Mrs. Delaford who supplied the lovely dresses and social introductions that would make the dream come true.

Until the conversation with Cal that led her to the Bible, Isa had simply gone along with the schemes of her mother and Mrs. Delaford, for she saw no other options for herself. She was poor, and she was female. She would never be allowed to run a plantation as Cal did or to pursue a meritorious career as Art and Wally were doing. Once, she had casually mentioned to her mother that she might like to become a teacher. Louise's reaction was sharp and short; no Dinsmore would ever be the hired governess for someone else's brats. "Get the idea out of your head right now," Louise had commanded. "You will marry well, and then you will pay some other poor woman to tend to *your* children."

So Isa went along, but she had her doubts. And as she pursued her study of the Bible, her doubts grew.

Isa became a frequent visitor to Ion that winter. At first, she went to see her cousins, particularly Missy and Molly with whom she could talk of art and literature — subjects vastly more interesting than fashion styles and the latest gossip that dominated Virginia's chatter. Elsie sometimes joined the girls in their conversations, and Isa began to seek out her elder cousin. Elsie knew immediately that her young cousin was troubled and confused, and she gladly made time for Isa.

"I remember once saying to Cal that he was a seeker," Elsie said to Isa one afternoon as they sewed together in Elsie's warm sitting room. Missy and Eddie had gone to the city with their father, Molly was napping, and the other children were playing in the nursery, so Elsie and Isa were alone. It was a cold day but bright, and sunlight filled the pretty room.

"I believe his searching is nearly done," Isa replied. "He has traveled a long road, but his faith is firm. He has opened his heart and accepted the saving grace of Christ."

"And he has no doubts?" Elsie asked.

"I do not think so," Isa replied. "Cal is like our Mamma in some ways. He tends to hold his feelings close. Yet I have never known him to be so happy. Not that he sings and prances," she added with a little giggle. "It is just that I can see a peacefulness in him that I've never seen before."

Elsie smiled. She understood what Isa was saying better even than the girl did. Elsie raised a quick, silent prayer of thanks to her Lord for Cal's salvation. Then she spoke to Isa again: "I sense that you are on the same road that your brother has followed and that you are a seeker. What is it you are searching for?"

Isa looked up from her sewing, and Elsie saw that tears were swimming in the girl's lovely eyes. Isa sighed heavily and said, "I am not sure. Oh, Cousin Elsie, I believe that there is something more waiting for me than the wealthy marriage and comfortable life my Mamma desires. I'm not like Virgy, you know. She will marry and be a wonderful wife and mother. I would like to marry, of course, but I feel that there is more that I must do, and yet I do not know the way."

"In your Bible reading," Elsie replied, "you may have come across this verse: 'The path of life leads upward for the wise to keep him from going down to the grave.'"

Isa smiled. "It is from Proverbs, is it not?"

"I can see that you are reading with close attention," Elsie said. "And in the same chapter is another verse: "The way of the sluggard is blocked with thorns, but the path of the upright is a highway.'"

Isa hung her head. "Then I must be a sluggard," she said, "for I seem to be wandering among the thorns."

"You misunderstand, my dear. God does not promise us an easy life in this world. The path is faith, and it leads to Him in this life and the next. That is the highway, and if we travel His path, we have a Friend who will be our constant guide and companion on the journey. When God is in your heart, Isa, He will lead you ever upward toward His Heavenly throne. You will make mistakes and know sorrow along the way, but when you love God, He forgives your errors and comforts you in grief. The sluggard is the person who makes no effort to find God's path, and that is not you, dear Isa."

"Does God speak to you, Cousin Elsie?"

"He speaks to all who will listen to Him. Yes, He speaks to me in many ways. It is the language of the heart, my dear, that we must listen to."

"Then He might speak to me?"

"If you accept in the depths of your heart that He is your Lord and Savior and if you give your life into His hands. You are troubled because you feel that you are not following your heart."

"That's true, Cousin Elsie."

"Yet who knows your heart better than your Heavenly Father? You can turn to Him and know that He is our 'ever-present help in trouble.'"

"My troubles seem so small. Not at all like what you have been through," Isa said. And then she reddened with embarrassment at having reminded Elsie of her grief.

Elsie's loving smile did not waver. "God doesn't make distinctions. He will be there for you every second of every minute of every day. You need only to turn to Him."

"Can it really be that easy?" Isa asked.

"Easy in the sense that God is always ready to hear you," Elsie responded. "But the decision to reach out to Him is yours alone. If you truly want to find your path, you must take the first step."

After supper with the family at Ion that evening, Isa was driven back to Roselands in the Travillas' carriage. She greeted her family, and then went straight to her room. Dropping her cloak upon the floor, she hurriedly took her Bible — which now showed the signs of much use — from its place on her bedside table and opened it at random.

As if an unseen hand controlled the pages, the book opened to the fifty-eighth chapter of Isaiah, and Isa read these words: "Then you will call, and the Lord will answer; you will cry for help, and he will say: Here I am."

She read on, her heart nearly bursting with happiness: "The Lord will guide you always; he will satisfy your needs in a sun-scorched land and will strengthen your frame. You will be like a well-watered garden, like a spring whose waters never fail."

She read the entire passage again, and then for a third time. "Here I am," she whispered softly. And once more she said the words aloud, "Here I am."

Then clutching her Bible to her breast, she closed her eyes and spoke in a voice that trembled with joy: "Here I am, Lord. My heart is yours. I put my life in your hands and my feet on your path. Please be my guide, Dear Father in Heaven. Please help me to do what is right and lead me toward your everlasting rest. I love you, Lord, with all my heart."

Isa spent many hours in conversation with her God that night. She told Him all that was in her heart. When at last she fell asleep, she dreamed sweet dreams of peace. And when she awoke the next morning, it was with a glad heart, for Isa knew that she no longer walked alone. A new life had begun.

CHAPTER

5

Travel Plans

*Like cold water to a weary soul
is good news from a
distant land.*

PROVERBS 25:25

Travel Plans

The Travilla family was gathered for breakfast one morning when a message of momentous import arrived in the first post. Edward was distributing the mail, as he always did, when he came to an envelope addressed to Molly. That Molly should get mail was not unusual; her brother Dick wrote her at least twice each week from Philadelphia. But Edward noticed that this particular envelope bore a New York return address and was written in a hand he had never seen before. He quickly passed the envelope to Molly and continued doling out letters and packages to the rest of the family, but his curiosity was aroused. Edward and Elsie now thought of Molly as more daughter than cousin, and whatever concerned her affected the Travilla parents as if she were one of their own.

Edward said nothing but watched Molly from the corner of his eye as she opened the envelope, withdrew its contents, and began to read. What a transformation he saw in her face! Her normally placid expression was replaced by a glow that came in part from a blush that spread across her cheeks. Her mouth opened and her eyes widened. She looked up from her reading and gazed straight at Edward, but she said nothing.

"What is it, child?" he asked, fearing the letter contained bad news of some sort.

Molly's lips moved, but no words came out, and Edward started to rise from his seat to go to her. But Molly finally found her voice and said, "It's a check. A check for one hundred dollars."

She held up the piece of paper for all to see. Now everyone was gazing at her in wonderment.

"It's from a publisher in New York," Molly managed to say. "They have bought my story for their magazine."

65

"Oh, Molly!" Elsie exclaimed. "That is wonderful!" And all the Travillas joined in offering their congratulations.

Edward, seeing that Molly was in a kind of shock, did rise now and go to her. Standing behind her chair, he gripped her shoulders and bent forward to kiss the top of her head. "We are so very proud of you, Molly. But come. You must smile for us, for this is a great achievement. I do believe you are the first in all our families to become a published author."

Edward felt her shoulders relax, as if the tension had suddenly been released. Molly turned to look up at him, and a broad smile spread across her face. Edward stood back and announced to the room, "A published author in the family!"

Molly demurred, "Not quite published, Cousin Edward, but they say here that the story will appear in their summer edition."

"And then the world will know what we know already — that our Molly is indeed a gifted writer and a remarkable young woman," Edward said, nearly crowing with pride.

"But what is the story about, Molly?" asked Eddie.

"Have we heard it before?" Harold wanted to know.

"No," Molly said. "It's a new story that I finished several weeks ago. I sent it to the magazine when I finished it, so there was no chance to test it on my family. I don't have a copy, so I guess you must wait to read it until the magazine appears. But I can tell you that my story is about a very large dog named Bruno who has an amazing adventure."

"Bruno!" Vi laughed. "You mean our Bruno?"

"Of course, she means our Bruno," Herbert said. "Is there any other Bruno fit to be the hero of a story?"

The merriment continued until it was time for morning devotion, and when Edward said his prayer for the people of Ion, he included special words of gratitude for Molly's first success.

Indeed, the sale of the story marked a major turning point for Molly. She had decided to become a writer and worked very hard at perfecting her craft. She had already sent several stories to various publishers. Although two of her poems had appeared in a local newspaper, her short stories had been rejected. Molly's disappointment had been deep, but through prayer and common sense, Molly struggled to conquer her fears and throw off her feelings of failure. *All writers face rejection*, she told herself, *but that doesn't mean they are not good writers. I will just have to work harder to improve my stories.* And work she did. She made herself write every day. When she was having trouble with a story, she didn't allow herself to dawdle and complain. She worked at something else — ideas for new stories, her translations of French poetry, and her journal. She would also read late into the night, studying the works and ideas of the great authors she admired. Six days of every week she worked, and on the seventh only did she rest.

Some may wonder what drove Molly to push herself to become a writer. After all, the Travillas had welcomed her into their home and family. She had every material thing she wanted and would always be well provided for. Elsie and Edward would see to that. Others might ask why a young woman doomed to life as a cripple should pursue a career so often marked by hurtful disappointments.

The truth was that for Molly, writing was a calling. Deep inside, she knew that it was what she must do. And there was also her determination to make her own way in the world. Not that she resented Elsie and Edward's charity. But when she had taken her anger and pain to her Lord and been relieved of those burdens by His love, she realized that God had also given her the talent to provide for herself and to contribute to the care of her sick mother. Molly trusted her Heavenly Father to guide her steps, and her first check for writing seemed to her a tangible proof that she was following the right course. She could have kept the money for herself, and no one would have thought her selfish. Instead, she divided her compensation into three equal parts. A third she sent to her grandfather at Roselands with a note telling him that she wanted it spent for her mother, Enna. A third she sent to Dick in a letter that explained her desire to assist him with the expenses of his medical education. The last portion she gave to Edward, and he accepted it without argument. The money itself meant little to him, but Edward understood Molly's feelings. This small payment (and there would be larger checks in her future, he was sure) reflected his young ward's growing maturity and her eagerness to take on the responsibilities of adulthood. He would not undermine her new confidence in herself by refusing her offer.

As the spring progressed, one member of the Travilla family found herself becoming increasingly restless. It was Vi, the adventurer of the family, who was always ready to tackle new challenges and travel to new places.

On a balmy evening early in May, she joined her parents as they sat on the veranda and enjoyed the fresh breezes.

"I believe I love Ion best in the spring," Edward was saying.

"And your garden is truly splendid this year, dear Husband," Elsie replied as Vi came to stand at her side. "I do not remember seeing the roses in better color. Do you not agree, Vi?"

"Yes, Mamma, I do. Papa's roses are very beautiful and smell so sweet, but —" Vi hesitated.

"But what?" Edward asked. "Perhaps you would rather I plant cabbages and carrots where the roses grow now," he teased. "They are not so sweet but much more tasty."

Vi giggled. "Oh, no, Papa. The roses really are just perfect. But I was wondering if we might be going away from Ion this summer. I mean on a holiday, a family holiday like we used to take."

"You are weary of your old home?" Edward asked in his teasing tone.

"Never, Papa," his daughter replied firmly. "But the weather will be hot soon, and we have not been to the beach in a very long time, and Rosemary and Danny have never even seen the ocean —"

"And our Vi has an itch to travel again," Edward said with a chuckle.

"I guess so, Papa," the girl replied. "I was embarrassed to ask for myself."

"Never be embarrassed to ask for what you want, dearest," Elsie said. "Your Papa and I will always listen carefully to your requests."

"And in this instance, I think our Vi has presented us with an excellent idea," Edward added. "What do you think, Elsie? We could take a cottage at Cape May, if one is still available. I can post a letter to the rental agent first thing tomorrow."

"Eddie will be finished with school in another two weeks, and if Vi and the twins will work very hard, we can complete their lessons by then," Elsie said. "We could depart at the end of the month and enjoy three months by the sea. Perhaps Papa and Rose would like to join us."

Vi, by now, was rocking on her toes. Her parents liked her idea. Then she had a worrisome thought. "What if there are no cottages to rent, Papa?"

"There are other beaches and other cottages, my dear," Edward said reassuringly. "You let me worry about finding a place for us."

"And Molly will go with us, won't she?" Vi asked.

"Of course, if she likes," Elsie said. "But we must present the idea to all the children and see if they approve. Shall we do that now?"

Edward was already on his feet. He gave his wife his hand, and she rose. Then he reached out for his daughter, and the three of them abandoned the night breezes to seek out the other family members. Within twenty minutes, all except the sleeping babies had been told of the holiday plan, and agreement was universal. The entire Travilla family would be traveling again.

<hr />

"I do think it strange," Louise said, "that Elsie should permit the family to take a holiday while they are still in mourning. It is not at all proper."

"Oh, Mamma, they have known such sorrow of late. Why begrudge them a holiday?" Isa responded.

"And Missy told me that they will accept no social engagements for the summer. That is proper, isn't it, Mamma?" Virginia added.

"I suppose so," Louise agreed without much conviction.

"Cousin Edward cannot leave Ion for several weeks, so Uncle Horace will accompany us on the steamer. Isn't it lucky that we can all travel together to Cape May?"

"Yes, lucky indeed," Louise said, though her tone conveyed less generous feelings. Louise and her daughters had been invited to travel north with Mrs. Delaford that summer. Their itinerary included a week in Philadelphia, followed by several weeks at a hotel in the Cape. Then they would proceed to a fashionable spa farther north. They were to meet Mrs. Delaford in Philadelphia where they would shop for "suitable attire" — Mrs. Delaford's phrase — for Virginia and Isa. As it happened, their schedule coincided with that of the Travillas and Dinsmores, so the families would travel as a group. This arrangement suited everyone except Louise, who preferred not to be under the watchful eye of her brother Horace. But since she could think of no reasonable objection, they would all depart from the city on one of the first days of June. The trip by steamship would take two days, and Louise resolved to hold her tongue for the duration.

Around her daughters, however, she was less cautious.

"I do not see why Elsie insists on dragging Molly along. What pleasure can the poor creature have being pushed about in that wheeled chair of hers and watching the others enjoy the sand and surf when she cannot?"

"Oh, Mamma!" Isa exclaimed. "Please stop calling Molly a 'creature' as if she were a pet on a leash. She is thrilled to be going. She will see Dick in Philadelphia, and you know that they haven't been together for more than a year. And she will benefit greatly from the sea air and sunshine at the Cape."

"Well, I agree with Mamma," Virginia said with a trace of the haughtiness she had inherited from her mother and grandmother. "When one is crippled like Molly, one must accept one's fate and not expect others to carry one hither and yon."

"She is not 'one,'" Isa said angrily to her sister. "She is our Molly, and she has as much right to some pleasure as you and I do."

Catching herself, Isa took a deep breath and softened her voice. "I'm sorry. I did not mean to shout," she apologized.

"I should hope not," Louise said. "Such displays of temper will earn you a bad reputation in society, my girl, and Mrs. Delaford, for one, will not tolerate impertinence. I will not have you offending our kind benefactress."

Virginia just laughed and put her arm around her sister's waist. "Isa meant no harm, Mamma," Virginia said brightly. "And neither she nor I would ever offend Mrs. Delaford. At least not till we are happily married and no longer need a benefactress. Then we can send her packing."

This last remark was not really made in earnest, for Virginia was not a cruel young woman. It did earn a smile from Isa and a dark look from Louise — just as Virginia intended.

"I should like to see you try to send Mrs. Delaford packing," Isa replied jovially. "I think you would have better luck marching the entire United States Army over a cliff than in moving Mrs. Delaford one inch from where she wants to be."

"Now that is a picture — Mrs. Delaford standing against the United States Army," Virginia laughed merrily. "What a battle that would be!"

Even Louise was amused by the image of her pompous sister-in-law facing down an entire army, and an unaccustomed smile played at the edges of her mouth. She instantly lowered her head to the sewing in her lap, hiding even this humble — and very human — emotional lapse from her daughters.

And so on a sunny morning in the first week of June, Travillas, Dinsmores, Conleys, and Molly Percival proceeded up the gangplank and boarded the steamship that would transport them on the first leg of their summer journey. The weather was perfection — a cloudless blue sky above and soft zephyrs rolling off the sea to cool the passengers. Once everyone had been shown to their cabins and unpacked their luggage, the family regathered on the steamer deck.

"Oh, bother!" Virginia pouted as she, Isa, and Missy took off on their first stroll around the ship.

"Is something wrong?" Missy asked with concern, for she could not imagine what might bother anyone on such a glorious day.

"Can you not see for yourself? Just look about us," Virginia replied petulantly.

Both Missy and Isa turned their heads this way and that to scan the ship.

"I see nothing but people enjoying themselves," Isa said.

"There is nothing amiss, Virginia," Missy concurred.

With a little gesture of impatience, Virginia whined, "Count the people. There must be a dozen women for every man on board, and most of the men I've seen thus far are older even than Uncle Horace."

Missy was somewhat perplexed by her cousin's remarks, but Isa laughed. "Don't tell me you expected to find a husband here, Virgy! Good gracious me, you have an entire summer to trap a man with your feminine charms. And we have only just left our first port."

"I have no need to trap a man," Virginia declared. "But you cannot blame me for hoping for the company of a *young* man or two on this voyage."

"Eddie is with us," Missy said innocently.

Virginia rolled her eyes and sighed, "Eddie is fifteen. He's my cousin and your brother. We cannot flirt with him."

Missy was a little shocked. "I don't want to flirt with anyone," she said. "I don't know how to flirt."

Isa took Missy's arm and bent close to her, speaking in mock confidence. "Virginia knows all about flirting, so you can learn from her if you are interested, Cousin, though I doubt you will be. I, on the other hand, seem wholly incapable of flirtation — much to my mother's regret and frustration. I have this dreadful habit of speaking what is on my mind, and I have never even once fluttered a fan or dropped a perfumed handkerchief to catch a man's eye."

Isa then raised her free hand to her brow in a melodramatic gesture. "Doomed, that's what I am. Doomed always to be taken seriously."

"Don't make fun of flirting, Sister," Virginia said with a grin and a toss of her pretty head. "No man wants to walk down the aisle with a girl who is always serious."

"Is that true?" Missy asked in astonishment. She would not turn eighteen until the following fall, and her experience of the rituals of courtship was almost nonexistent.

"Do not let Virginia lead you astray," Isa said. "Of course, men marry serious women. And they marry flirtatious women, and they marry smart women and silly women. And women marry smart men, and they marry silly men. I believe that women and men must be true to their natures, but Virginia and I do not exactly see eye-to-eye on this matter. Still, we've agreed to disagree with good humor. Haven't we, Virgy?"

"We have," Virginia replied with a sweet smile. "But will you please stop calling me 'Virgy'? It was alright when we were children, but we are grown now, and I wish to be known by my adult name."

"I'm sorry," Isa said contritely. "It is only the habit of many years, and I will try very hard to break it."

The young ladies continued their stroll, and as they came around to the opposite side of the deck, Virginia emitted a barely audible gasp. "Look there," she whispered. "The young man in uniform standing by the railing. It is Lieutenant Brice. He's an Army officer I met at a party last summer. Quite handsome, don't you think?"

"Quite," Isa replied with little interest.

They walked on until they came to the soldier, and Virginia stopped.

"Why, I do believe it is Lieutenant Brice!" she declared in a voice that suddenly contained the drawl of the deepest South. "How charming to encounter you here. But perhaps you do not remember me?"

"Of course, I do," the young man said, bowing from the waist. "It is the lovely Miss Virginia Conley of Roselands Plantation. And the pleasure is all mine."

He took her gloved hand and gave it a quick kiss. And then Virginia introduced Isa and Missy. A momentary glint — unnoticed by the young women in the bright sunlight — came to the soldier's eye when he heard the name "Travilla."

The foursome chatted for a while; then Isa and Missy politely excused themselves to continue their walk. But Virginia lingered, saying, "I should like to hear more about the lieutenant's career in the Army. I will join you two in just a bit."

Virginia and the handsome officer were still standing by the railing, talking with animation, when Horace Dinsmore happened to observe them. He did not interrupt, but turned in the opposite direction. Horace knew of the solider — knew a good deal more than Lieutenant Brice could have guessed — and he wanted to find his sister.

Louise was resting in a deck chair, her straw hat pulled low over her face, when Horace approached.

He got directly to the point. "Your daughter is associating with a young man whose reputation precedes him," Horace declared bluntly.

Raising the brim of her hat, Louise demanded, "Which man? Which daughter? What are you talking about?"

Horace sat on the chair next to hers. "I have just seen Virginia with an Army fellow named Brice. Do you know him?"

Louise thought for a moment, then said, "Algenon Brice? Why, yes, we met him last summer. Very attractive and quite gallant. How nice that Virginia has found a friend on this voyage."

"He comes from a good family, Louise, but he does not do his parents proud. He is known to be a wild and reckless man, given to gambling and drink. I advise you to intervene."

Louise sat upright and glared at her brother. "I will do no such thing," she declared in a steely voice. "I have no intention of embarrassing a gentleman in that way."

"You need not confront him," Horace replied, adopting a gentler tone. "Just take Virginia aside and inform her about the man. She can avoid his company for the remainder of our trip." Then he added in words Louise could not misinterpret, "If you fail to intervene, then you will force me to take action."

Louise deeply resented her brother's threat and thought it yet one more proof of his high-and-mighty piousness, but she knew better than to oppose him. "I will do as you request," she agreed. "I just hope Virginia is not too disappointed, for I have noticed how few men of a companionable age are on board."

"She would be more disappointed to learn that her own reputation has been tarnished by public association with a man of his ilk."

In fact, Virginia was not at all upset when her mother told her what Horace had said. Virginia had little real interest in Lieutenant Brice beyond passing the time. As they had conversed earlier that day, he had revealed himself to be rather a bore, for his questions all seemed to dwell on the Travillas and Missy. Virginia could be an astute judge of character when she paid attention, and it had become clear to her that Mr. Brice had set his cap for her wealthy cousin and looked upon Virginia as merely a means to his end.

"It's fine with me to ignore Mr. Brice," Virginia said readily, much to Louise's surprise. "There are much better fish in the sea, if not on this ship, Mamma. I did not know of the things Uncle Horace told you, but I suspect Mr. Brice of less than honorable purposes. I hadn't heard about gambling and drinking, but I feel certain he is a fortune hunter."

"But he is a gentleman from a fine family," Louise protested.

"A fine family with no money," Virginia laughed. "I'm sure that the prospect of a union with the Travillas crossed his mind the minute he learned Missy's name."

"Missy? But she's a mere girl."

"She will soon be eighteen, Mamma. She is incredibly beautiful, like her mother, and educated, and she will inherit great wealth one day. I know that she is naïve, but she is not a little girl anymore. It is kind of Uncle Horace to protect me — don't shake your head, Mamma. His concern was genuine, and I appreciate it. But I am much less in need of his sheltering than Missy is. The world is full of men like Lieutenant Brice, and Missy is ill-equipped to read their minds and motivations."

They were alone in their cabin and the dinner bell rang as Virginia was speaking. She quickly put a brush to her hair and smoothed the ruffles on her dress.

"Isa will be waiting for us in the salon," Louise said as she walked to the cabin door.

But Virginia needed one more minute. She was adjusting a gold pin on her blouse as she said, "Leave this matter to me, Mamma. Please tell Uncle Horace that I shall spend no more time alone in the lieutenant's company. I need not be rude to Mr. Brice, for Missy and Isa will be my constant companions. We shall be as thick as thieves for the rest of the trip — Isa and Missy and I — and no man shall intrude upon our merry trio."

Louise looked in some amazement at her charming daughter. In truth, the mother thought of Virginia as her frivolous child — always laughing and taking nothing too seriously — but for the first time she recognized another quality. Strength. Virginia had seen through the unimportant Mr. Brice, but she had seen more, and in her own way, this merry, flirtatious girl had resolved to champion her innocent cousin against a schemer's advances.

"Should I mention your observations to Horace? About Missy?" Louise asked.

"No need for now," Virginia said as she finally secured the pin and gave her hair one last pat. "Uncle might think you are just getting back at him."

Virginia fairly danced to the narrow door, opening it for her mother and then following Louise into the hallway that led to the dining salon. "Let me be Missy's guardian angel for a while," Virginia said brightly. "I shall enjoy the role, I think."

CHAPTER

6

Storms Ahead

I would hurry to my place of shelter, far from the tempest and storm.

PSALM 55:8

Storms Ahead

The second day at sea dawned calm and clear, and the families emerged from their cabins early and energetically. After breakfast, Virginia organized a card party in the salon with Isa, Missy, and Molly. Elsie, Eddie, and Vi joined Horace for a morning stroll. Then Vi settled into a deck chair with the book she was reading, while Eddie and the twins went off for a very special adventure. The captain had taken a shine to the boys at supper the previous evening and promised them a tour of the steamer. Horace was invited, too, and with the first officer as their tour guide, the little group spent the entire morning inspecting the steamer's workings from stem to stern. Herbert and Harold were enthralled with the giant pumps and pistons and the massive boilers in which the steam that powered the ship was generated. Eddie, who had always been fascinated by machinery, had countless technical questions, which the first officer happily answered in great detail.

Elsie played with her little ones for several hours, until the children's nurse took Danny and Rosemary for their naps. Elsie then decided to indulge in some reading of her own — a new novel that had arrived just before the family left Ion — so she got the book from her cabin and went to join Vi on deck. What a surprise to see that Vi was engaged in animated conversation with a man. Because his back was to Elsie, she could not see his face as she approached, and she was somewhat disconcerted that Vi would so readily strike up acquaintance with a stranger.

Seeing her mother, Vi stood and waved. The man stood as well, and when he turned around, Elsie recognized him immediately. It was Lester Leland, the nephew of the

81

Travillas' neighbors and dear friends who lived at Fairview. Lester was from the North but had spent the recent winter months with his Southern relatives. He was an artist — quite poor, it was true, but to Elsie's critical eye, very talented as well.

"Why, Mr. Leland, we did not know you were on board," Elsie declared as she extended her hands to him for a warm greeting. "We didn't see you at supper last night."

Lester lowered his head slightly and smiled sheepishly. "I'm afraid water travel is not natural for me. I remained in my room yesterday until I could get my sea legs."

"Were you sick, Lester?" Vi asked impishly.

"Vi!" exclaimed Elsie. "That is a most impolite question."

"It's alright, Mrs. Travilla," Lester said with a laugh. And turning to Vi, he added, "No, Miss Inquisitive, I was not sick. Just a bit green about the gills, as they say."

"Well, sit down with us, and tell us about your travels," Elsie said. "Are you on the way home to see your parents?"

Lester explained that he was, indeed, going to have a brief visit with his family, but he would be staying for most of the summer in Philadelphia. He was to study with an excellent painting teacher there, and he would support himself by giving drawing lessons to the daughters of several prominent families in the city.

The three chatted and were joined a while later by Missy and the other girls. Elsie found herself highly impressed by the young's man intelligence and self-effacing manners. He was not at all abashed by so lively a group of young ladies, yet he maintained a certain reserve that was entirely correct. Elsie invited him to share the family's table at dinner and for the rest of their brief journey, and Lester gratefully agreed.

There was another traveler who was far less impressed by the young artist. From a position some distance from Elsie and the young people, Lieutenant Brice observed them with mounting fury. The lieutenant had plotted to engage Virginia's attention that day and through her, to become better known to the wealthy cousin. Now he had been thwarted by a rival, and a poor one at that. Judging by Lester Leland's attire — the ill-fitting jacket with what appeared to be a green paint stain on the sleeve, the clean but frayed shirt, worn trousers, and unfashionable boots — the lieutenant concluded that the fellow was clearly a bounder. *But what possible interest could the girls and Mrs. Travilla have in such a shabby person,* Brice wondered as he jealously observed the cheerful gathering. *I've heard that the Travillas are big on religion. Perhaps the scoundrel appeals to their tenderhearted mercy. But that does not explain Virginia Conley's attentiveness. She's no Bible-reading churchgoer,* the lieutenant thought, *yet she deliberately ignores my attempts to catch her eye, and see how she laughs at whatever that bumpkin has just said.* He continued to watch for some minutes more, then decided to retreat and rethink his strategy. Reminding himself that anger was a poor substitute for cunning, he decided to wait for his chance to approach the young ladies. *After dinner, perhaps*, he told himself, *for surely those silly girls will tire of the pauper by then.*

Lester Leland, however, did not go away, and Lieutenant Brice had to content himself with the company of some older ladies whom he knew. He cleverly pumped the ladies for information about the Travillas and Missy in particular.

When he had learned all he could, he excused himself and went below — locating a cabin where several men of less genteel repute were gambling at cards.

That afternoon, the temperature began to rise and became so uncomfortable that strolling the decks brought no comfort. The oppressive heat was unrelieved because the breezes off the sea, which had been so pleasant, died away. Conversation was also stilled by the heat as passengers sought out shady spots and tried to cool themselves with their fans. A gathering of clouds late in the afternoon promised to bring temperate air again, but Horace quickly recognized that the clouds most likely portended a storm.

He was standing by the railing, looking at the sky, when Vi found him.

"Do you think it will rain, Grandpa?" she asked.

"I believe it may, my dear," Horace said. "And blow as well. Do you see how the clouds have darkened? They may signal a thunderstorm coming our way."

A sudden gust struck them, rippling Vi's skirt. Horace had to clutch his hat to keep it from blowing away. Then it was still again, but Horace could feel the increasing roll of the steamer beneath his feet.

"Is it dangerous, Grandpa? A storm at sea?" Vi wanted to know.

"It can be, but don't be afraid. Remember that our Heavenly Father watches over us wherever we are. He brings the storms just as He brings the quiet."

Vi slipped her hand into her grandfather's. "May I stay with you and watch the clouds?" she asked.

Horace looked down into her face and smiled his assent.

Eddie and the twins soon gathered around Horace and Vi, all watching as the sky darkened and the thunderclouds moved swiftly toward them. They could see flashes of light in the clouds, and the gusts of wind became stronger. The sea seemed to change color, from bright blue to a dark, silvery gray like old pewter, and the waves grew in size and force, hitting the side of the ship like heavy hand-slaps. The children grasped the railing to steady themselves and felt the ocean spray on their faces. So mesmerizing was the sight of the oncoming storm that only when large, cold drops of rain began falling did Horace shepherd his little flock back to the shelter of the large salon. He was surprised to hear himself shouting over the wind as he directed the children to take cover from the rain.

Elsie, holding baby Danny in her arms, was sitting on a long banquette in a corner of the salon. Missy was seated on one side of her mother and the children's nurse, with Rosemary in her lap, on the other side. In her wheelchair, Molly was close by Missy. Louise and her daughters stood at a window, watching as streaks of lightning tore through the gloom outside. The rain popped against the glass of the window, and just as Horace and the children approached the families, a loud clap of thunder sounded. A startled cry escaped Virginia, and the Conley ladies hurried away from the window to find seats around the banquette.

The storm was upon them now, and all round the room families huddled together — faces pale and ears pricked to catch the voices of the crew and the sounds of hurried feet tramping the decks. Amid the crashing of the thunder, the roar of the winds, the pounding rain, and the creaking of the ship as it struggled forward in the roiling sea, the passengers could hear no more than the occasional fragment of a shouted order from the officers and crewmen. Though the words were unintelligible, it was somehow comforting to hear the seamen and know that they were doing their jobs.

As the storm's fury increased, the steamer was tossed from side to side, and the few pieces of furniture that were not bolted to the floor skittered about the room. "Grab that!" Horace shouted to Eddie as a small food cart hurtled their way. "Hold it down so that it does not strike anyone." Eddie seized the cart, and Harold pulled a length of rope — a souvenir of his morning tour — from his pocket. The boys lashed the cart to the leg of a table.

Horace had taken a chair, moving Molly's wheelchair to his side and holding it firmly. Molly, whose face was ashen with fear, nevertheless managed a small jest. "I'm sure the other passengers thank you, Uncle Horace. Should my chair roll free, I could do them more harm than this storm."

"Are we in danger of striking the rocks, Papa?" Elsie asked her father in a brief moment of quiet.

"I think not," he replied. "The storm is from the northwest and blows us toward the sea rather than the shore."

At that instant, a terrible cracking sound assaulted their ears, followed by a roll of thunder louder than any they had heard yet. The whole ship shuddered, and several people in the room were thrown to the floor. A man's panicked voice rose high above the screams and cries — "We've struck ground! We'll all be drowned!"

Horace shouted out, "Be quiet! We haven't struck ground! The ship is sound and the crew is brave! Remain steadfast, everyone, and trust in the Lord. Keep your heads, as Jesus admonished His disciples in the storm. Comfort one another and put your faith in our Lord! He alone can rebuke the winds and waves and restore the calm!"

His powerful voice was so full of authority and confidence that the other passengers soon settled their cries and began to help their fellow travelers. A great many prayers were said in the next few minutes.

The Travillas' nursemaid, whose name was Christine, hugged little Rosemary close and began to croon softly. Her song was an old hymn, and her voice sweet and clear as she sang the words, "Jesus, Savior, pilot me, o'er life's tempestuous sea." Violet, who huddled against her Cousin Isa, started singing along, and soon all the family was joining in. The song spread about the salon. It was not a heavenly chorus, but no one cared about the quality of the singing. Everyone in the room raised their voices in unison, drawing strength from their shared prayer. They sang through the hymn once, and then again. They held close to one another and sang until their voices almost drowned out the whistling wind and raging sea.

At length, a woman exclaimed, "Listen, everyone! The storm is dying!"

The singing ceased and indeed, the noises of the storm were lessening. The intervals between thunderclaps were longer. The dreadful creaking, which seemed to signal that the ship was breaking apart just minutes before, now sounded like mere echoes. The ship still rolled on the rough waves, but the motion felt more rhythmic, and the passengers knew that the steamer was no longer battling the sea but moving in stride with it.

Tears of relief and pure joy were shed by one and all. Laughter, too, was heard throughout the room, as the passengers marveled at what they had just passed through. The storm had come up just before suppertime, and now stewards walked among the passengers, offering to get tea and sandwiches for everyone — most of the evening meal having been dashed to the kitchen floor at the height of the storm. Horace insisted that all his family have sweetened tea and something to eat, for he knew that the shock and fear of their experience would fade with nourishment. Then he asked his family to clasp hands and join in a prayer of thanksgiving to the One who had brought them through safely. When he came to the end of the brief prayer, his family responded with grateful amens — all save little Rosemary who had drifted into sleep as the storm subsided. She woke, rubbed her eyes, and looked about her. "Is it over?" she asked sleepily. Assured by Christine that the storm had passed, Rosemary sat up straight, clapped her hands, and added her own merry "Amen!"

The storm was ended, but the danger had not passed. Lester Leland had been in his small cabin when the storm rose. He had tried to get to the salon, but a crewman had sharply warned him not to go on deck. So he remained alone for the worst of it. Now he made his way to the others, nimbly negotiating his way through the busy seamen who worked on deck.

Entering the salon, Lester looked around until he spotted his friends. He strode toward them and was warmly greeted by everyone. He answered all questions about his own whereabouts during the storm, noting that he regretted not seeing the chaos, for it surely would have made excellent subject matter for a painting.

The stewards arrived with cups of hot tea and plain but delicious sandwiches, and as the family was eating —

finding themselves ravenous after their adventure — Lester managed to pull Horace aside.

"Mr. Dinsmore, I fear that we may be in for more trouble," Lester began, speaking low so that others might not hear. "I overheard some of the crew as I came up from my cabin, and there is some problem with a fire in the hold."

"The ship is carrying a cargo of cotton," Horace said.

"Ah," Lester responded, "that explains the men's worries. While in my cabin, I heard and felt a mighty crack that surely was a lightning strike. It nearly threw me from my bunk. I believe the mast was hit and a fire started in the rear."

Horace's face betrayed his worry at this news. He knew how difficult it is to control any fire at sea, and the presence of a full load of raw cotton greatly increased the danger. He immediately decided to keep his family above deck until he learned exactly what was happening and the extent of the hazard.

"Say nothing as yet," Horace told the young man. "This steamer is well equipped with lifeboats and vests, but we must not cross any bridges till we reach them. Come, have some tea and sandwiches with us."

Lester, who had experienced no twinges of seasickness even at the height of the storm, suddenly felt a wave of queasiness. "I would like a cup of tea, sir," he said to Horace, "but I think I shall forgo the food."

It was about twenty minutes later that the first officer came to the salon to make an announcement. The captain sent his regrets for any inconvenience, the man began, but requested all passengers to stay in the lounge for the time being. The captain expected a second storm during the night. The ship would weather a new storm as well as it had come through the first, but only as a precaution, the stewards would be distributing life vests to the travelers.

No, no, there was little cause to worry, the officer assured the questioning passengers. The vests were only a wise precaution. Food and drink, blankets, and pillows would be provided, and the passengers were asked to remain where they were just until the captain gave permission for the return to their cabins. With luck, the officer added, they would escape the bad weather and reach the port of Philadelphia on schedule in the morning.

The voices so recently raised in song dissolved into a cacophony of anxious questions and fearful speculations as soon as the first officer had taken his leave.

Horace's family stayed generally calm, but he could see that they were frightened.

"Can this ship endure another storm?" Isa asked.

"It is one of the newest and best constructed steamers of the line, as Eddie, the twins, and I saw today," Horace said. "I have great confidence in the captain and his crew as well."

"I saw them working just now," Lester added, "and they are clearly skillful and well-ordered seamen."

"Let's not anticipate troubles, children," Elsie admonished. "The officer said we may well escape another storm. But whatever happens, we are in God's hands."

"And the winds and waves obey Him," Missy added in a small voice.

Louise had risen from her chair and was pacing the floor near another group of passengers that included Lieutenant Brice and his gambling companions. The men were deep in conversation and paid no attention to Louise, but she happened to hear some of what they were saying. Her face lost all color as the import of their words sank in, and she rushed back to her family, drawing Horace aside.

In trembling tones, she whispered to him what she had heard. "They say the ship is on fire — that there is fire in the hold and the men can't control it. Oh, Horace, I do not want to die here!"

"Calm yourself, Sister," he said, taking her shaking hands in his. "We must trust the captain and his crew, and not the gossip of disreputable men. I beg you not to spread this story and scare the others. You must be strong if danger lies ahead."

Louise drew in a deep breath and bit down on her quivering lip. In a matter of seconds, she composed herself and assured her brother that she would keep the gossip to herself. "But you must promise me one thing, Brother," she said earnestly. "Whatever happens to me, you will see that my girls are saved. I could not survive if Isa or Virginia were lost."

Gently, Horace stroked her hand as he said, "We are none of us lost if God is with us, Louise. Can you turn to Him now? Open your heart to Him, and He will carry you through. Will you pray for our safe deliverance, dear Sister?"

"I will try," she replied softly. "Perhaps Isa will help me."

"Yes, your younger daughter is a fine Christian. Both your daughters have your strength to endure. Go to them now, and if you cannot begin your own prayer, ask Isa for the words. Speak to your Lord and Savior now, for He has said, 'where two or three come together in my name, there I am with them.'"

Some time passed and nothing happened. Rumors of the fire had circulated, causing great anxiety among the passengers, but the stewards had calmed fears, and after about an hour or so, people began asking when they might return to their cabins. They were restless now that the danger had passed and wanted to resume their normal activities. They chatted and laughed and complained about their confinement, and the volume of voices in the large room rose so that no one heard the tapping of raindrops at the windows.

Then, more suddenly than the first storm, the second hit the steamer. The ship lurched sideways, and thunder crashed overhead. The steamer rolled from side to side, and because the passengers were unprepared, a number of people were thrown about. One man fell against a table, and blood began to pour from a wound on his head. A steward rushed to help.

Rain pelted the windows, and thunder rumbled deeply. Children clung to their mothers and cried. The courage that had gotten the passengers through the first storm was weaker now, and similar thoughts passed through many minds — surely the ship could not withstand another battering. The rumor of the fire was reignited, and terror of burning or drowning swept the room.

Horace and his little band, however, maintained themselves with prayer. Each person quickly put on a life vest, and Horace helped Molly into hers. As he was fastening the strap, Molly grabbed his hand and said, "If the worst happens, Uncle Horace, tend to the others. Save them first. My useless body will do nothing but slow you down."

"Dear girl," Horace declared, "I would never leave you behind. Do not think such a thing."

"I am being realistic, Uncle," she said firmly. "If it comes to a choice between my life and Missy or Vi or any of the others, they must come first. Promise me that, Uncle, and that you will tell Dick not to grieve for me, for I have gone on to my Heavenly Father."

Horace did not protest, though he knew that he would do all in his power to restore his niece to her brother. He quickly finished with the strapping and took his seat beside her, holding her chair with one hand and her hand with the other.

The storm continued for some time, but when the first wave of fear had subsided, the passengers realized that this was not so violent as the earlier tempest. The rain was extremely heavy, but the ship did not toss so wildly nor did the thunder roar so loudly as before. A few people cried and moaned, but most grew silent — listening to the storm for signs that it was abating.

And it did. The rain slowed and softened until it was no worse than a spring shower. The lightning paled, and the thunder faded to distant echoes. Relief spread among the passengers, but they did not rise, and what conversation there was, they conducted in whispering tones. Twice now, they had endured the fury of sky and sea, and they dared not predict what might come next.

Little Danny had slept through the entire ordeal in his mother's arms, and Elsie gazed into her child's placid face with wonder. She recalled a verse from First Peter: "Like newborn babies, crave pure spiritual milk, so that by it you may grow up in your salvation . . . ." Then silently she formed a prayer: *Oh, Lord, grant me the faith of a child and the courage to face whatever storms life may hold with the perfect trust of my sleeping babe. Shelter all my children from tempest and storm in the knowledge of Your divine love. Be ever our strength and our comfort even in the valley of the shadow of death. I love You, Lord, and give myself into Your hands.*

The captain came to the salon a short while later. He was rain-soaked, but his dripping uniform did not detract from his inherent dignity. Every eye in the room was instantly riveted on him.

A small smile came to his lips as he began speaking. "I believe that all danger is passed, and we will proceed to our destination on calm seas. I understand you heard rumors of a fire in the hold. The rumors were true" — gasps came from several people — "but the fire is now out. It did not reach our volatile cargo — thanks to the intervention of our Heavenly Guardian. The second storm doused the flames at deck level, and my men were able to stop the burning below deck. I believe the fire is completely out, but I have posted a crew below to watch for any signs of renewal. The ship has suffered some damage, but the engine rooms were far from the blazes, so there will be no disruption of our journey."

Many smiles broke out in the room and not a few prayers of thanksgiving were spoken. Then the captain went on, "Most of you may return to your cabins now, but some of the rear compartments have taken on water and smoke. Those of you affected should remain here for the rest of the night, and my crew will retrieve your luggage. Any losses you may have as a result of the storm will be compensated by the steamship company.

"Truly, I regret what you have been through this night. Take pride in yourselves, for you have all behaved with great fortitude. Now, I will be glad to answer any questions you may have."

There was a quick flurry of queries, which the captain answered completely and candidly. But most of the passengers were too tired for intense discussion, so the captain was able to depart after about ten minutes, and the passengers who could return to their quarters began to drift away. Horace guided Elsie and Louise and their families to their rooms and then retired to his own.

Only Lester Leland and a few others remained in the salon, for their cabins were located in the damaged area of the ship. Lester found a pillow and blanket and stretched out on the banquette so recently occupied by the family. He said a fervent though silent prayer of thanks and then tried to sleep. But two thoughts tugged at him. One was his concern for the portfolio of drawings and paintings that he had left in his room. He was taking the portfolio to his teacher, and it contained the best examples of his art. Could these precious items have escaped the water and smoke? The second thought was vastly more pleasant. In his mind's eye, Lester could see a face — the loveliest face he had ever known — and he imagined the portrait he wanted to paint of it. It occurred to him that no work of art he had ever done was so beautiful as that face, and he wondered why he had not noticed its perfection before. With the vision of large hazel eyes, ruby lips, alabaster complexion, and gleaming brown hair pushing all his cares aside, he finally dozed off.

CHAPTER

7

Happy Reunions

*It is God who arms me with strength
and makes my way perfect. He makes
my feet like the feet of a deer; he
enables me to stand on
the heights.*

PSALM 18:32–33

*N*ever had Elsie or her family been happier to stand on solid ground! The steamer reached port early the next morning, and the passengers, still shaken by their harrowing experience, hurried ashore. The first familiar face they saw was Dick Percival, and the Travilla children surrounded their cousin and began talking in excited tones of their adventure.

"A huge storm" — "waves as high as the ship" — "lightning and fire" — their words came flooding out in excited tones as they talked over one another, and poor Dick could make neither heads nor tails of what they were saying.

Fortunately for the dismayed young man, Horace interrupted the babble after a few moments. He was pushing Molly in her chair, and when Dick saw his sister, he instantly bent to hug her and kiss her cheeks.

"Oh, Dick," she exclaimed, "I thought I might never see you again!"

"But what happened?" he asked.

"A storm like nothing I have ever seen," she declared, taking his hands in hers and gripping them with unexpected strength. "It struck the ship last evening, and was followed by a second storm. God was truly with us, Brother, and I thank Him with all my heart that He has allowed me to behold your face once more."

Dick raised his dark eyes quizzically to his uncle.

"We've had a narrow escape," Horace said, "and we shall tell you all about it over breakfast." Turning to Eddie, Vi, and the twins, he commanded, "Hush now, children. We must collect our luggage and make our way to the hotel. There will be plenty of time to tell your tales when we have settled in."

Dick had three carriages waiting, and it was not long before all members of the family party were installed in their hotel. Rose and Rosie were awaiting them there, for they had come to Philadelphia a week before to visit with Rose's family. Once rooms were sorted out and bags delivered, the family reunited in the dining room for a hearty breakfast, and the children had their opportunities to regale their relatives with all the details of the storm. The story was repeated often over the next ten days — to Mr. and Mrs. Allison, to Adelaide and Edward Allison and their children, to various servants and hotel staff, and finally to Edward Travilla, who joined his family near the end of their Philadelphia visit.

With each retelling, the story of the storm at sea seemed to gain strength. The waves became higher, the fire more threatening, and the worthy captain and crew elevated to grand, heroic dimensions. Elsie and Horace corrected the more extravagant elaboration, but in general they allowed the children to indulge their imaginations. Better, the adults decided, that the children remember the incident as an adventure than with fear and dread.

The Philadelphia stay was enjoyable for all. The Dinsmores and Travillas spent many happy hours with the Allisons. Adelaide and Edward Allison hosted a lovely party for the family in their new home. Edward Allison was now well on his way to becoming one of the leading industrialists of the time, and the new house — a mansion, really — reflected his growing prosperity and social position.

Mrs. Delaford arrived several days after the family and soon had Louise, Isa, and Virginia in tow. The redoubtable matron was far less impressed by tales of storms at sea than by the many fashionable shops in the city. Louise and

Virginia happily fell into Mrs. Delaford's busy schedule of dressmakers, shoemakers, milliners, and so on. At heart, Isa had little interest in this whirl of fashion and finery, but she had determined to be compliant. She did, however, manage to politely excuse herself on several occasions and enjoy some of the sights in the historic city with her cousins Dick and Molly. One particularly beautiful day, Dick took the young women on a tour of his college, and Isa found herself feeling unexpectedly drawn to Dick's world of classrooms and libraries.

The reunion of Molly and Dick was perhaps sweetest of all. The brother was truly awed by the changes he saw in his sister. It had been almost two years since they were last together, and in that time Molly had grown both lovelier and more mature. She had the beauty of her youth, but a wisdom and serenity that were far beyond her years. The two had many long talks, and Dick was constantly astonished by his sister's easy confidence and quick mind. He introduced her to several of his classmates, and they, too, found her to be an exceptional companion.

"Maybe I should not say this," one of Dick's friends remarked one day when the two young men were alone in their dormitory, "but your sister is one of the most extraordinary young women I have ever met. I expected her to be bitter or depressed about her condition, for I know you said that her paralysis is permanent. But she seems hardly to notice it. When we all went to supper and the theater last night, I forgot entirely that she was confined to that chair. We see so many people with similar handicaps here in medical school, and my attitude has always been to pity them. But your sister has done much to change my way of thinking. Maybe I will be a better physician as a result of meeting her, for she has shown me that physical disadvantages are no impediment to the growth of heart and mind."

When Dick relayed his friend's observations to Molly, she was both pleased and thoughtful. "I had not considered myself capable of inspiring anyone like that," she said. "Yet if your friend has learned something about people with handicaps, then I am most happy," she said.

"You have much to teach, Molly," Dick said. "We all take the gift of good health and strong bodies too much for granted. I see so much illness and suffering, and I have to admit that, like my friend, I am inclined to pity our impaired patients and to think them helpless."

"Needing help is not the same as being helpless, Brother," Molly replied. "I need help, and for a long time, I thought that made me pitiful. You may tell your kind friend that I have struggled with bitterness and the darkest depression. It was thanks to Cousin Elsie and Cousin Edward and Uncle Horace that I began to see myself not as a useless creature but as a child of God. In His eyes I am no different from the able-bodied. He looks into my heart — and the hearts of all His children — without prejudice."

"But you must feel angry sometimes," Dick said. "I know that I resent what has happened to you."

"Oh, don't, dear Brother," she implored. "Resentment and bitterness are far more crippling to the soul than the inability to use one's legs. When I think about it, I naturally regret my condition. Yet I often wonder — if I had not fallen down the stairs because of those silly shoes, what would I be today? Would I be part of so loving and generous a family as the Travillas? Would I be writing and actually publishing my work? Would I be able to help you and our mother? Would I have received the greatest gift of all — my faith in God's all-encompassing love?"

Dick smiled and took her hand. "We have both been brought to Him through tragedy, so you are right, Little Sister. If He had not interceded in our lives, I would doubtless be a rakish riverboat gambler by now and you a brainless social butterfly."

Molly tossed her head and laughed brightly, and for a moment, Dick saw in her face the child she had been, full of energy and wild enthusiasm.

"I doubt our fates would have been quite so dismal," she responded.

"Just promise me, Molly," he said with sudden earnestness, "that you will never lose your joy in living."

"How can one help but love life," she replied, "when it is the path that leads us to eternal peace in the house of our Father?"

"Have you ever considered writing about your own experiences?" Dick asked.

Molly thought for a moment then said, "Yes, but I am not ready yet. I still have much to learn before I can do that. I keep upon my desk at Ion a quotation from the great poet William Wordsworth. He said, 'Poetry is the spontaneous overflow of powerful feelings: it takes its origin from emotion recollected in tranquility.' I am still gaining the tranquility, Dick. I write stories about others now and use what I know of life to make my fictions real for readers. But my own story? I consign my feelings and experiences and observations to my journal only, while they are fresh. But the art of writing, I believe, lies in the ability to distill strong feelings in such a way that other people can read and feel them as well. Someday I shall write about my life and yours and the lives of all the people who mean so much to us. But to be great, a writer must capture feelings that everyone can share. I am not yet ready for that, although each story I write brings me a little closer."

"Will you let me read your journal someday?" he asked.

"Possibly," she smiled. "But I warn you. It is mere ramblings and questionings. In the future, perhaps, when my life has run its full course, you may read my journal and make some sense of it."

Their Philadelphia sojourn passed all too rapidly, and by mid-June the families had packed again and continued on to their summer retreat in Cape May. The Travillas and Dinsmores had rented separate but adjacent cottages on the beach. The Conleys and Mrs. Delaford took up residence in a local hotel just a few blocks away. They would journey farther north to an expensive watering place in New York during July.

Getting away from Ion proved to be restorative for all the Travillas. The younger children played to exhaustion each day on the sandy shores, and the parents gave them freedom to pursue their interests, though always under the watchful eye of themselves or Christine, the efficient nursemaid. Eddie soon found friends of like age among the other summer residents and was busy from breakfast to supper with his new pals. Missy was often in the company of her mother and grandmother, but she and Rosie enjoyed many afternoons on the beach, reading or talking or exploring the natural environment so unlike the farmlands of home. Molly sometimes joined them, though she devoted most of her time to her writing.

The family did not accept any formal social invitations that summer, but they did occasionally join some old friends for intimate and casual gatherings. For Elsie and Edward both, it was good to be with their contemporaries — parents like themselves who knew of the loss of their darling girl and offered loving support.

Isa contrived to escape as often as possible from her mother, sister, and Mrs. Delaford. Even an hour or two with Elsie, Rose, or her cousins seemed to revive the girl's spirits, for Isa was having considerable difficulty keeping both her temper and her tongue in check. The social activities planned by Mrs. Delaford were endless and stretched Isa's endurance to the limits.

"All I hear is how this young man is so handsome and that one so wealthy and yet another one of such good family. I do believe that Mrs. Delaford has recorded the incomes and pedigrees of every eligible bachelor in this entire country!" she declared one afternoon when she arrived at the Travilla cottage, finding Elsie alone on the porch that overlooked the sea. Isa sank down beside her cousin on the comfortable couch and continued, "Virginia thinks it is all just grand, and she enjoys being the belle of the ball. I feel as if I were a sack of potatoes or a slab of bacon being put out for sale. Surely, there is more to finding a husband than this mad round of tea parties and dances and boring chitchat all the time," she sighed with exasperation. "Why do I need a husband anyway if all that matters is the size of his bank account and the loftiness of his family tree? And do you know who showed up at the hotel? That insufferable Lieutenant Brice! He hinted at wanting to pay a visit here, but I told him that you are in mourning and not receiving any guests for the entire summer. Oh,

Cousin Elsie, I know that was indelicate of me, and I hope you forgive me. But I just could not bear the thought of that foppish fellow showing up at your door."

Elsie easily forgave Isa and counseled the young woman to have patience. Perhaps the move to the New York spa would ease the pressure. Citing a verse from the twelfth chapter of Romans — "Be joyful in hope, patient in affliction, and faithful in prayer" — Elsie said, "I know how trying this is for you, Isa, but you must take your woes to the Lord."

"I feel so shallow praying to Him about my discomfort," Isa replied in choked tones. "Mamma is only trying to do her best for me, yet I get so angry with her and can barely stop myself from talking back. I hate dressing up and going to parties! What could be more trite and trivial? Yet I am so ashamed of feeling this way when there are so many people who suffer so much every day. I should be grateful that my problems are no more important than what shoes to wear with which dress."

Isa was crying now, and Elsie held her close, rocking her as if she were a child. "God is not ashamed of you, Isa dear. He understands your feelings and wants to help you. He does not think your feelings trivial, and neither do I. I would never advise you to rebel against your mother or Mrs. Delaford, but I do know that your instinct is correct. Marriage is instituted by God. It is sacred and precious. Yet I am afraid too many people these days think that marriage partners can be bought and sold, as you said. You will find the patience to endure if you share your feelings with your Heavenly Father. He is your model of real love and faithfulness. Keep Him in your heart, and nothing can shame you."

"He will not think me so very selfish?" Isa asked as she brushed the tears from her cheeks.

"Open your heart in prayer, and He will do something much more valuable for you," Elsie said softly. "He will help you to know when you are being selfish, and He will support you in every step you take on the path of honor. You are caught in a dilemma, Isa, which is not at all trivial. You want to honor your mother and Mrs. Delaford and Virginia, yet you also want to remain true to the highest ideals of true love and marriage. Believe me that I know how you feel, for I was once torn in a similar way by my own feelings. You must not be afraid to ask for God's help. He will show you the way to manage your feelings and hold true to your principles."

"It is not always easy to be a good Christian," Isa said with a wry little smile.

"It is easier if you remember that you cannot hide from your Heavenly Friend. Throw off your shame and fear. Approach Him with an open heart, and He will take your hand and guide you aright. No matter how small a problem seems to you, nothing is too small for Him."

When Isa left the cottage that day, she felt a good deal better. God would always walk with her, just as He walked with all who believe in Him, through her trials as well as her triumphs.

Other visitors came to the seaside cottages that summer. Dick made the trip from Philadelphia several times and spent long weekends with Molly and his relatives. Two of Adelaide's children, who were near Missy and Eddie in age, came for a week to stay with their Aunt Rose and Uncle Horace. During their visit, the young people enjoyed excursions planned by Horace to local historic sites and a wonderful, final bonfire and picnic on the beach arranged by Rose and Rosie.

Elsie had invited Lucy Carrington Ross and her family to visit as well, but Lucy sent her regrets in an excited note. Her daughter Gertrude was engaged! The wedding was planned for September, and Lucy dearly wanted Elsie and Edward to attend. But there were so many preparations to be made that Lucy could not get away from her home in New York for even a few days.

Lester Leland, on the other hand, did respond with the sincerest gratitude to the invitation Elsie sent. Knowing that Lester could not afford to travel on his own, Elsie included a round-trip railway ticket in her letter to the young art student. He came for three days in August, fitting into the family as comfortably as an old friend. He played ball games with Eddie and his friends. He taught Vi and the twins how to skip flat pebbles over the sea. He also helped Missy with some sketches she was attempting, showing her techniques to capture the look and feel of foaming waves and fleecy clouds. She was an apt pupil. When she showed her drawings to her father, Edward had an idea. Since Lester would be returning to Fairview that winter, perhaps the artist might tutor Missy and Molly in drawing and painting. Edward made his proposal in a private meeting, offering payment that Lester at first refused as too generous.

"Do not underestimate yourself," Edward replied seriously. "You have a fine talent, and the girls will benefit greatly from your tutelage. And someday, when your works hang in the great museums, we will all be extremely proud to say that we knew you when."

Lester was quickly convinced and agreed to the plan, though in truth neither money nor future fame weighed much in his decision. He returned to Philadelphia and his studies, though his mind was now focused on his return to the South.

And so the summer progressed — warm and healing for everyone. For all but one of the Travillas, their departure from Cape May in the first week of October was a sad one. Only Missy packed her bags with a sense of anticipation, though she was a little surprised at how much her interest in the arts had recently grown.

8

Women of Marriageable Age

*A good name is more desirable
than great riches; to be
esteemed is better than
silver or gold.*

PROVERBS 22:1

Women of Marriageable Age

From Molly's journal, dated November 19, 1875:

I have neglected my journal for too many weeks, but there is a reason. I was commissioned by *The Ladies' Friend* — a magazine in New York that has published several of my stories — to write a series of articles about the lives of women in the South today. It is a most fascinating subject, and I spent the entire summer and most of the fall focused on this work. The articles have now been submitted to the editor, and I have a bit of time to return to my story of myself.

We are home again, having returned to Ion last month. Our summer beside the sea proved most invigorating for the whole family, in spite of its nearly disastrous beginning. It was not, however, so felicitous for everyone. I refer to Lucy Carrington Ross, Cousin's Elsie's dear friend from childhood. I have, of course, met the Rosses many times since first moving to Ion, for they often visit here. I even based one of my articles for *The Ladies' Friend* on Mrs. Ross's mother, Mrs. Carrington — an estimable woman now in her eighties — and her daughter-in-law, Sophie Allison Carrington, who is the younger sister of Aunt Rose. I did not use their names in my article, but created characters much like them — gentlewomen who suffered terrible losses of husbands, sons, and brothers in the war and yet have struggled and rebuilt their lives for the sake of their children.

Lucy Ross, on the other hand, has lived in New York with her husband since she married. They have six children. The eldest is Phil — Philip Ross, Jr. — who is now in business with his father. The second child is a daughter, Gertrude, who is twenty, I believe, and the center of this story. The information comes from correspondence between Cousin Elsie and Mrs. Ross. I have decided to record the story here because of my interest in the lives of women in our country today and our hopes for the future. In the tale of Gertrude Ross and her marriage, I think I see a message that all young women and their mothers would do well to heed. Someday I may draw on the details to write a fiction with a moral.

I recall all the Ross children, from Phil and Gertrude to the youngest, as lively and bright but dreadfully spoiled. Their mother seemed never to tell them no. Even my poor Mamma, though indulgent and even neglectful, exercised more discipline than Mr. and Mrs. Ross and would never tolerate bad manners in public. Cousin Elsie has said that Lucy seems afraid of her children, fearful of losing their love and affection if she denies them what they want. That may explain why Mrs. Ross excuses her children's unmannerly behavior and threatens them with punishment but rarely carries through.

At any rate, this story begins when a letter arrived at Cape May announcing Gertrude's engagement to a man named Mr. Larrabee of St. Louis. He was not known to Mr. or Mrs. Ross and was a good many years older than Gertrude, but he was also wealthy and apparently devoted to Gertrude. So the Rosses approved of the planned nuptials. According to the letters Mrs. Ross wrote, the wedding was to be a sumptuous affair and the costs were enormous.

At first, Mrs. Ross's letters were filled with little beyond gay recountings of fittings for Gertrude's immense trousseau, Gertrude's choices of silver and china, Gertrude's lavish menu for the wedding banquet, Gertrude's plans to decorate the church and the house with white roses, and so on. Clearly, no expense was being spared in order to gratify Gertrude's wishes. She even had her wedding gown redesigned and resewn *three* times until she was satisfied with the bustle and the train.

Then came a letter with a different tone. Mrs. Ross meandered about the subject — as Cousin Elsie says she has always done — but the gist was that the mother was having doubts about her daughter's motives for marrying. Cousin Elsie received another letter just two days later in which Mrs. Ross flatly stated her fear that Gertrude was marrying for wealth and security and that on Gertrude's side there was no love for the intended spouse. Cousin Elsie was clearly troubled by this news and wrote a most kind and loving letter in return, advising her old friend as best she could.

No more was heard until a day in August when a beautifully engraved invitation to the wedding of Gertrude and Mr. Larrabee arrived at our cottage. Cousin Elsie and Cousin Edward discussed attending the affair, but they decided not to. They might have made the journey had the wedding been an intimate occasion, but the loss of Lily was still too fresh a wound and participating in so large and festive an event was too much for them. Elsie wrote a lovely letter of regret to Mrs. Ross, and a handsome wedding gift — a sterling silver tea service — was sent to New York from the Travillas and the Dinsmores.

Elsie's Great Hope

The next letter came two weeks later — not quite a month before the wedding date. Mrs. Ross was distraught. A man had arrived at their home one night, urgently requesting to speak with Mr. Ross, and now the whole wedding was off. The man was a business acquaintance of Mr. Ross. He was from St. Louis but had been staying in California. He learned of the planned wedding only on his return. This man — and what a true friend he was — had boarded the next train and proceeded directly to New York, traveling night and day without stop, to bring news to Mr. Ross. Mr. Larrabee, whom the man had known for many years, was indeed wealthy, but his riches had been acquired through the worst kinds of fraud and bribery. Mr. Larrabee had once been jailed in the West for blackmail, and there was talk among some of the businessmen of St. Louis that he might soon stand trial for a more recent series of underhanded dealings.

One can but imagine Mr. Ross's fury. He sent word to Mr. Larrabee immediately, canceling the wedding and forbidding the man to have contact with Gertrude or any member of the family. Gertrude was hysterical — devastated by the humiliation of calling off her wedding. The entire household was in chaos. Mrs. Ross's letter to Cousin Elsie, which was barely legible in places and spotted with tears, indicated her own fragile state of mind.

If this were the end of the story, it would be sad but not so unusual. And one would be content that, despite her embarrassment, Gertrude Ross was saved at the last minute from a terrible fate. But another letter in Mrs. Ross's large, childish handwriting arrived ten days later. The wedding was on again, only the groom would be a Mr. Hogg and not the felonious Mr. Larrabee. This Mr. Hogg was a well-to-do gentleman who had long shown interest in Gertrude and her younger sister as well. Mrs. Ross did not explain how the switch was made — and it would be unkind to guess — but the wedding did take place in September, just as Gertrude wanted, with only one alteration. According to Mrs. Ross's last letter, Gertrude walked down the aisle with head held high, and though many of the guests surely wondered why the groom was not the man they expected, none dared say a word.

I have no right to judge the participants in the tale — except Mr. Larrabee. We have since heard that he is to face a judge and jury in a Missouri court of justice and is likely to spend his remaining years in prison.

But in writing my articles on women, I have found myself questioning the roles we play in this modern world. There can be no doubt about the importance of marriage and motherhood — two blessed states that are denied me now. But is that all we are suited for? It is often said that women's brains are too weak for serious learning and serious thought and that we are fit only for rearing children and keeping house. But I cannot accept such nonsense. I turned again to the book of Galatians today, finding the verse that has been so meaningful to me. "There is neither Jew nor Greek, slave nor free, male nor female, for you are all one in Christ Jesus." If God draws no distinction, should not His children follow His way?

Elsie's Great Hope

From Molly's journal, dated December 12, 1875:

I have pondered deeply over this question of women of late. First there was the story of Gertrude Ross, now Hogg, which I recorded here earlier. Now we have received the news that our darling Rosie is to be wed next spring to a wonderful young man who asked for her hand last summer. I am, I suppose, at that age when marriage is the center of so many thoughts and activities. I am truly joyful when I hear that someone I love like Rosie has found the right person to be her partner for life. Cousin Trip, who married not long after my accident, is so happy in his marriage, and I am confident that Rosie has chosen just as wisely.

But there are times when envy enters my heart — knowing that I shall never have a husband to love and be loved by, that I cannot have children of my own to hold and care for and raise in the faith that means everything to me! When I see the happiness of others, jealousy threatens me and might overtake me if I could not call upon my Lord for strength.

I have talked about my feelings often with Cousin Elsie, and she is both sympathetic and realistic. She has never considered marriage to be the chief goal for women, and she is raising her daughters to expect more of themselves. She says that a young woman who exercises her mind and her individual talents is far better prepared for marriage and motherhood than one who worries only about courtship and the attentions of young men. A woman who counts on marriage to end all her problems is in for a rude awakening. I asked her how she came to this way of thinking, and Cousin Elsie gave much credit to her parents and to Cousin Edward. Elsie told me that her husband was considered quite a radical in his youth, for Edward never accepted the idea of "female inferiority." I must say that the encouragement my Cousin Edward and Uncle Horace give me as I pursue my writing is unwavering. When my stories were first rejected for publication, it was Cousin Edward who taught me to see that rejection can be a step forward, not a step back. I shall never forget his exact words: "If the rejection is merited, learn from it. Evaluate your work and ask yourself what can be improved. If you are willing to be your own hardest critic and not to blame others for your failures, then you will achieve the success you deserve."

From Molly's journal, dated January 3, 1876:

I am not the only one troubled by this question of "a woman's place." I had a long visit with Isa yesterday, and she finally told me all that happened to her and Virginia last summer, after they left Cape May. As always, Mrs. Delaford made every decision, with Aunt Louise following in her wake. Isa did manage to enjoy some of her time in New York. The resort they visited was located in a beautiful forested area near the Hudson River, and there were daily opportunities to ride on horseback through the countryside and explore the natural environment. Since most of the other ladies' attention was directed to the various parties and dances held each evening, Isa often found herself free during the days. She says that she read voraciously, renewing her acquaintance with the great books, polishing her Latin, and taking up the study of Greek.

Virginia, however, seems to have thought of nothing but finding a husband. She has always been flirtatious and that is part of her charm. But pressured increasingly by Aunt Louise and Mrs. Delaford, Virginia's flirting became rather desperate. Isa expressed concern that her sister has earned a reputation for mindless teasing and shallowness among the many young men they met. As the summer wore on, Isa began to worry as well about Virginia's health. Virginia attended every party, dancing with every available man until the last note of the orchestra was played. She forced herself to be always gay and witty. Yet the more she shined in public, the more wan and depressed she was in her private moments with Isa.

"Virginia gives the impression of wanting to marry well because she has not money to support herself and is too lazy to work," Isa told me. "But I understand now that she is really frightened of being alone. She has a good mind and a good heart, but she lacks all confidence in herself. I have tried to talk with her about the only love that endures for all eternity and the true joy offered to her by our Lord. But she tells me she cannot think about religion now, that she will consider her spiritual life once she has secured earthly happiness with a husband and children."

Aunt Louise has been quite put out with both girls this winter. She is afraid that Mrs. Delaford's interest in them will wane. Aunt Louise is angry with Virginia for trying too hard, and at Isa for not trying hard enough to make good matches that will meet Mrs. Delaford's standards. Isa joked that in her mother's eyes, Virginia is the "rock" and she is the "hard place."

Isa confided to me that she has definitely decided to become a teacher, but she has not told her mother yet. Isa is investigating all her possibilities first, and deep in her heart, what she really wants is to go to college! Oh, how I hope that her dream may come true and she can take her place in the halls of learning.

I am not sure what makes a good marriage. To my Mamma, it was romance. To Aunt Louise, it is material security. To Gertrude Ross Hogg, I suspect it is wealth and social position, and Mrs. Delaford seems to regard matrimony as a matter of proper breeding — as if poor Virginia and Isa were two Kentucky thoroughbreds. For Cousin Elsie and Cousin Edward, the main ingredients are clearly love, respect, and shared faith. If marriage were open to me, I would choose the path of the Travillas. But marriage is not possible, and I must guard against envy and self-pity and reach out for other goals. As Cousin Elsie has told me many times, God has a purpose for each and every one of His children. With Him as our guide and companion, every life is rich and full.

CHAPTER

9

A Centennial Birthday

*Do nothing out of selfish ambition
or vain conceit, but in humility
consider others better
than yourselves.*

PHILIPPIANS 2:3

*E*ighteen seventy-six was to be a special year for all Americans. From the Atlantic coast to the Pacific, people were preparing to honor the first one hundred years of their nation's history, and the biggest celebration of all would be held in the birthplace of American democracy — Philadelphia, Pennsylvania.

Naturally the Travillas and the Dinsmores, who had so many close connections in the "City of Brotherly Love," planned to be there. The Dinsmores would stay with Rose's family in their city house. Edward and Elsie had made arrangements to rent a large and elegantly furnished house convenient to Fairmount Park, which was to be the site of the country's first international exhibition. They would be in residence from May through September, returning to Ion just six weeks before the Philadelphia Exhibition drew to its close.

The only disappointment in their plans was that Aunt Chloe and Old Joe would not accompany them. Joe, as spirited as ever, was too crippled with arthritis for travel, and Aunt Chloe could not be tempted to leave his side. She was to assume management of the household at Ion during the family's absence, and Mr. and Mrs. Daly would take up their duties as tutor and housekeeper in Philadelphia.

There was a great deal of excitement among the residents of Ion and The Oaks in the weeks preceding the trip — and not only on account of the Exhibition. On a brilliant day in mid-April, Horace was father-of-the-bride for a second time, as he and Rose gave their daughter Rosie in marriage to Anthony Lacey, the son of friends who occupied a plantation not many miles away from The Oaks. As he had with Elsie,

Elsie's Great Hope

Horace felt a bittersweet mingling of joy for his daughter and new son-in-law and sadness that the last of his children was leaving his house. That Rosie would be living close by lightened his burden considerably, as did the fact that he approved wholeheartedly of Rosie's choice of husband.

The wedding itself was the perfect expression of Rose Dinsmore's exquisite taste. No detail was overlooked, yet the atmosphere was as friendly and relaxed as if the marriage were being celebrated in a country cottage. The guest list was limited to family and close friends, as the bridal couple wished, and at Rosie's special request, even Enna — accompanied by her nurse — was in attendance. The bridal party included Missy, Vi, Isa, Virginia, and Betty Johnson as bridesmaids and young Rosemary as flower girl. Eddie was a groomsman, as well as the Conley brothers. But to everyone's delight, the first bridesmaid down the aisle was Molly Percival, her flower-bedecked wheelchair pushed by her brother, Dick.

At the height of the wedding reception, the newlywed Laceys left for their honeymoon in France amid a shower of rice and good wishes. With a gentle reminder from Rose that he would someday be asked to walk another "daughter" down the aisle — for Betty and Bob Johnson were as dear to the Dinsmores as their own children — Horace quickly wiped a tear from his eye and joined in the merriment of his guests.

Two weeks later, both families and their entourage boarded the train for Philadelphia — the suggestion of a boat trip having been soundly rejected by all. And soon they were settled into their separate households to await the official opening of the Exhibition by President Ulysses S. Grant.

A Centennial Birthday

The first day drew the largest crowd of any event ever held in the United States. Although rain had fallen the previous day and night, the sun appeared on the morning of May 10 — just in time for the pealing of the bells in Independence Hall, which announced the start of the celebration. By nine o'clock in the morning, some 100,000 people were gathered at the park, and police had their work cut out for them as they tried to keep order. When the gates at last opened, eager men, women, and children swarmed into the park grounds and filled the plaza between the Main Exhibition Hall and Memorial Hall for the outdoor opening ceremony. A large orchestra began to play patriotic music, and soon the official speeches began — though hardly anyone could hear what was being said. Finally, President Grant addressed the large assembly, declaring the Exhibition open, and a chorus of more than a thousand singers burst into the "Hallelujah Chorus."

Edward Travilla and his older children were there for the historic opening, and their stories of the first day — the deafening cheers and shouts of the jostling crowd, the waving banners and flags, the bursts of military artillery, the opening of various exotic exhibits from countries as far away as Japan and China — all the sounds and colorful sights of the day soon became part of the family's history, to be passed down through many future generations. Luckily, the Travillas decided to leave the park early in the afternoon and missed the rains that drenched and muddied the thousands of people who remained until the first day's closing moments.

Elsie's Great Hope

The Exhibition drew visitors from all parts of the country and from many foreign lands. The Emperor of Brazil had been there for the opening ceremonies, and myriad languages were heard each day by visitors as they crowded the many exhibition halls. The Exhibition celebrated not only the first century of the United States but also the country's first great international spectacle.

The Travilla children attended the Exhibition frequently — sometimes with their parents but more often with Mr. Daly, who employed the exhibits to teach everything from agriculture to fine art. Each of the youngsters had a favorite site. Eddie was drawn again and again to the famous Corliss Engine — the huge steam engine that powered all the machinery in the Exhibition. Herbert favored the Prismoidal Railway, a kind of railway car shaped like a prism that crossed a deep ravine on a single track. Harold constantly asked to ride the glass elevator to the top of Sawyer Observatory, a 185-foot tower that offered spectacular views of the entire exhibition. Vi preferred the Horticultural Hall with its jungle-like displays of plants and flowers from the far corners of the world. And Missy was attracted to the Ladies' Pavilion, which had been built entirely with money raised by American women.

The Travillas deliberately chose a house that was larger than their needs so that they might entertain friends and relatives who visited the Exhibition. Their first houseguest was a valued friend who had shared a past adventure with them. Yes, it was Elsie's jovial Scots cousin, Ronald Lilburn, who was touring the United States with his sons Malcolm, age twenty-two, and Hugh, two years younger. What fine, strapping young men they were — each as tall as his father and each blessed with the same radiant smile.

A Centennial Birthday

The Lilburns arrived in Philadelphia about a week after the opening, and they went first to the Allison home where they were warmly greeted and directed to the Travilla house. There they were met at the door by Elsie, whom Mr. Lilburn instantly swept up in a great bear hug. "Oh, it's fine to see you again, lass," he laughed. "Eight years it's been, boys, since I laid eyes on Cousin Elsie, and she has grown even more beautiful since last we met."

Elsie returned the hug, though not so forcefully. After being introduced to the Lilburn brothers, Elsie bade them all to follow her to the dining room, where the family would be gathering momentarily for the mid-day meal.

"Did you get my letter, lass?" Cousin Ronald asked.

"Indeed we did," Elsie replied. "We were not sure on which day you would arrive, but rooms are ready for you, and we insist that you stay here with us."

"But that is too kind," Mr. Lilburn said graciously. "The last time I visited, I arrived out of the blue, and you took me in. I do not expect such hospitality again."

Elsie laughed happily. "Never was a guest more welcome, now as then. Has your father told you about his part in our battle with the Ku Klux Klan?" she asked the sons.

"He has mentioned it, ma'am," Malcolm replied.

"If mention is all that he has done, then we shall have a great tale to tell you," Elsie promised.

At that moment the door swung open, and Edward entered. His countenance lit like a lamp when he saw who was there. Edward and Mr. Lilburn engaged in a manly embrace, followed by introductions to Malcolm and Hugh, which were repeated several times as the children appeared for dinner.

Elsie's Great Hope

The servants were much surprised by the great rounds of laughter and other peculiar happenings at the table that day, for the Travillas were normally quite sedate when they dined. A servant girl excitedly reported back to the kitchen staff that the pot had actually whistled "Yankee Doodle" when she was pouring coffee for one of the Scotsmen!

The children retired to the parlor with their parents and cousins after the meal, and at last everyone heard the full story of the battle with the Klan and Cousin Ronald's decisive role in it. Rosemary and little Danny understood little of what was said, but they laughed and clapped hands along with everyone else when Edward told how Cousin Ronald had tricked the Klansmen by pretending to be the U.S. Cavalry. Then Mr. Lilburn entertained the youngsters with more examples of his ventriloquism.

The Lilburns accepted Elsie's invitation and had soon unpacked their bags. After supper that evening, the whole family took the newcomers on a carriage ride around the Exhibition grounds, and Missy and Eddie happily agreed to accompany Malcolm and Hugh on a return visit the next day.

The Lilburns were just the first of many who stayed with the Travillas in the next few months. Dick Percival, who was in his final year at medical school, was a frequent guest — to Molly's delight — and stayed overnight on those rare occasions when he did not have hospital duty. Sophie Carrington and her brood came north to stay with her parents, and Sophie spent many hours with Elsie. In June, Mr. Lilburn and his sons left for a tour of the Adirondack Mountains and New England, but would return in late August. Their places were quickly taken by Lucy Ross, her daughter Kate, and Mr. and Mrs. Hogg. Vi soon made friends with Kate — an energetic girl, willful at times but full of fun and ready for adventure. The Hoggs were perfectly polite, and Edward found that Mr. Hogg, who was in the import and export business, was a very pleasant companion and quite well-informed when the subject turned to international affairs. Gertrude, however, seemed unimpressed by her husband, and though the couple were always courteous to each other, there was a distance between them that had the effect of chilling everyone around them.

Lucy and her group stayed for three weeks, and near the end of the visit were joined by Phil Ross — Lucy's very handsome and very conceited eldest son. Phil soon made his intentions clear; he was far more interested in renewing his acquaintance with Missy than in the attractions of the great Exhibition. They had known each other since childhood, but Missy rarely thought of Phil when he was not present. Phil, however, had given a great deal of thought to Missy. Some years earlier, he had determined to woo her and win her when they were of an appropriate age, and now the time had come — in his mind at least.

Phil contrived in every way to be with Missy, but he was not alone in his pursuit. Several young men began calling on the Travillas. One was a cousin of the Allisons who was employed as an accountant by Edward Allison. Another was a distant relative of old Mrs. Carrington, a lawyer in the city who had met the Travillas at a party at the Allison home. If truth be told, Malcolm Lilburn also cherished special feelings for Missy and fully intended to get to know her better when he returned to Philadelphia.

And then there was Clarence Augustus Faude, the son of a new friend of Elsie's. Mrs. Faude was a charming matron and shared many interests with Elsie. The two met through a mutual acquaintance, and Elsie immediately took a liking to the lady. Mrs. Faude, whose home was in Kentucky, was refined and intelligent, an entertaining and witty conversationalist, and a Christian. But as Elsie soon discovered, Mrs. Faude had one blind spot — her only child whom she always referred to as "my darling Clarence Augustus." According to Mrs. Faude, Clarence Augustus was nothing short of ideal in every way, as brilliant and sophisticated as he was handsome and debonair.

Elsie and Edward began to grow curious about this paragon of male virtues, and in mid-summer, they were able to meet him at last. Clarence Augustus, who had been away on a short tour of Europe, arrived on one of the hottest days of July and was introduced to the Travillas at a supper party Mrs. Faude held in his honor that evening. Mrs. Faude had not exaggerated his physical attributes, for Clarence Augustus was a remarkably handsome young man. His style of address was most cultured and his conversation revealed the excellence of his education. He was a courteous host to one and all and paid special attention to Missy, who was the only other unmarried person at the gathering.

During the carriage ride home from the Faudes' hotel, Edward teasingly asked his daughter's impressions of Clarence Augustus.

"He certainly is as well featured as his mother said," Missy replied, "but you have always taught us not to be misled by appearances."

"Quite right," Edward said.

"Did you form an impression of his character, dear?" Elsie inquired.

"An impression only, Mamma, but certainly not sufficient to draw conclusions. He seemed nice enough, and his conversation was quite interesting. And he was a very considerate supper partner. Beyond that, I have no opinion."

"Well, I feel sure we will be seeing more of Clarence Augustus Faude," Edward declared in a hearty manner.

Indeed, Clarence Augustus became a frequent guest at the Travilla home, with his mother and without her. He arranged a number of activities to include Missy, Vi, and Eddie — visits to the new Philadelphia zoo and tours of the historic sites around Independence Hall. He occasionally accompanied the Travillas and Mr. Daly on their rounds of the Exhibition, though Clarence Augustus had little liking for the dust and noise of the fair and even less taste for the crowds of "common people" he encountered there.

But Clarence Augustus, with his mother's blessing, had determined to court Missy Travilla. She met most of his lofty standards — rare beauty to complement his own, grace in form and manner, education, and wealth. There was perhaps too much of the casual style of the Southern aristocracy about her, but that could easily be corrected, he thought. A little polish was all that was needed. Under his influence, she would soon enough be transformed into the grandest of ladies. In the young man's mind, he had found a suitable match, for he appraised Missy as a young woman with almost as many gifts as himself.

Missy welcomed Mr. Faude into her home just as she welcomed every new friend. She thought him to be a pleasant companion, especially knowledgeable about art and music. But then, Missy found something to like about each of the young men who paid calls. The young accountant turned out to be a wonderful dancer and an excellent partner at dance parties. The lawyer was also a student of history, and from him she learned much about the past of Philadelphia and its role in the founding of the nation.

By instinct, Missy tended to overlook flaws in others and search for their positive qualities. In all her relationships, she seemed oblivious to any motives other than friendship. That any of the young men she knew might consider her for a life partner was the furthest thought from her mind.

Others in the family were less naïve. Vi proved herself most astute, for she sized up Mr. Faude upon first meeting him, although she kept her opinions to herself for some time. Then one day, she and Missy and Eddie were occupied in planning a garden party that the Travillas would host for the young people. They had decided on a number of games to play at the party and written down a list of foods and drinks that they would suggest to their mother — Eddie insisting that the party table should include the new root beer he always enjoyed at the Exhibition, as well as the traditional lemonade. Then the young people got down to their guest list.

"I suppose we must include Mr. Faude," Vi said with a heavy sigh.

"And why not?" Missy asked, for her younger sister's tone surprised her.

"Oh, he's alright, I guess," Vi said, "but he always seems to be looking down on other people. I hate the way he pats me on the head as if I were the family dog and then acts as if I were invisible to him."

"We should have brought Bruno," Eddie said, "so Mr. Faude could have a real dog instead of just your head to pat."

"I expect that he is just unused to the company of people your age," Missy said nicely. "He is an only child, you

134

know, and not accustomed, as we are, to people younger than himself."

"But if you married him, how would he act around your children?" Vi demanded. "Would he just forever pat their heads and send them off to play by themselves?"

"Marry him?" Missy exclaimed in shock. "Whatever made you say that, Vi?"

"Well, that's what he wants," Vi declared defensively. Then she giggled, "He doesn't come here to see me and Eddie. That's for sure!"

When Missy replied that Mr. Faude came to visit with their parents, Eddie snorted.

"Missy, you cannot be so blind," Eddie said with a broad grin. "Clarence Augustus would marry you tomorrow if he could. As would Mr. Chase and Mr. Blanton and Phil Ross for that matter."

A bright flush came to Missy's cheeks at her brother's words, and she managed to say only, "Don't be foolish, Eddie."

"We're not trying to tease you, Sister," Eddie responded in a kind tone. "But what young man wouldn't want to marry my beautiful sister?"

"Just don't marry Mr. Faude," Vi said with a pretty little pout. "He's handsome and he's smart, but not nearly so handsome or smart as *he* thinks. You've got lots of beaux to choose from."

"But I have no intention of choosing anybody, not for a very long time," Missy replied firmly. "I have no intention of leaving my family until I am much, much older."

"Then you won't marry Clarence Augustus?" Vi asked.

"No."

"Phil Ross?" Eddie chimed in.

"No."

"How about Mr. Chase?" Vi asked, turning the conversation into a game.

"No."

"Mr. Blanton?"

"No," Missy replied, stifling a giggle.

"How about —" Eddie had to think for a moment. "How about Malcolm or Hugh Lilburn?"

"They're our cousins," Missy declared. "But no, even if we were not distantly related."

"What about Harry Carrington? He's a nice boy," Vi asked, thinking of Sophie's eldest son.

"He's very nice, but no."

"What about Archie Leland?" Eddie laughed.

"Even if he weren't three years younger than I, no," Missy said, joining in the laughter.

"Then Lester Leland?"

Missy hesitated for the shortest part of a second, then she said, "It's time to stop this silliness and get back to our work. Mamma expects to see our guest list this afternoon."

Reminded of the task at hand, Vi and Eddie turned to their pencils and sheets of paper and began hurriedly writing down the names of their friends. Missy, however, was caught in a thought. Was Lester Leland still in Philadelphia? He had not been able to visit Fairview that winter as he hoped or to teach drawing lessons at Ion, so she hadn't seen him for a year, although she thought of him more often than she admitted to herself. Was it possible that he was still studying in the very city where she now dwelled? *I wonder how we might be able to locate Mr. Leland*, she mused. *I'm sure Mamma and Papa would enjoy seeing him again. They both like him very much.*

CHAPTER

10

A Chance Encounter

In his heart a man plans his course, but the LORD determines his steps.

PROVERBS 16:9

A Chance Encounter

*T*he heat in August was so intense that the Travillas considered retreating to cooler climes for the month. But more guests were scheduled to arrive at their temporary home. The Lilburns were returning, and Elsie's Aunt Lora and several of her children were coming north to see the Exhibition. Elsie and Edward could easily have left the household and hospitality to the Dalys, but the Travillas were not the kind of people who ignored their responsibilities as hostess and host.

The family did, however, decrease the frequency of their visits to Fairmount Park and engaged in activities less exhausting than tramping about the massive Exhibition. Mr. Daly conducted his classes in a "schoolroom" under the leafy shade of a large maple tree in the garden and organized field trips to historic sites that were both educational and sheltered from the sun. Weekend visits to the country home of Adelaide and Edward Allison provided respite from the crowded city, and the Travilla youngsters spent many hours playing in the brook where Elsie had once waded and made little boats of leaves to sail on the rippling waters.

Missy discovered the pleasures of the Academy of Fine Arts, where painting and sculpture of the finest quality appealed to her aesthetic sense and the cool setting allowed hours of viewing in relative comfort. One especially hot day, Mrs. Faude and her son invited Missy and Eddie to accompany them to the gallery, for Clarence Augustus was particularly eager to see a new installation of landscape paintings. They planned to lunch at a restaurant in the city and spend the entire afternoon at the Academy.

139

Clarence Augustus, whose knowledge of art was extensive, could not refrain from lecturing the young Travillas and his mother about every work they saw. He informed them about the history and reputation of each artist, the materials used in the creation of each piece of art, the significance of color and composition. He extolled the use of light in American landscape painting and contrasted American art to English, French, and Italian styles. He also knew the value of each work — the price it would bring in the marketplace. His commentary was interesting, and his mother was, as always, his most attentive listener, hanging on every word Clarence Augustus uttered as if it were pure gold. Eddie was attentive, too, for a time, but after about an hour, he wandered away to see some Western paintings that were more to his taste.

Missy found herself growing annoyed, and she struggled against the feeling. Not that she was bored by Mr. Faude's remarks. There was no doubting the depth of his understanding, and he was an engaging speaker. But Missy had learned from her parents that art was to be experienced with the emotions as well as the intellect. She preferred to gaze upon a painting or sculpture until it came to life for her. She believed that true art lay in the artist's ability to draw the viewer into the experience he had represented in paint or stone. When Missy admired a work of art, her reaction came first from her heart — not from knowing how many brushstrokes the artist used.

They came to a painting of a storm at sea, which tugged at Missy. At she looked into its depths, she could feel the power of the cresting waves, the threat of the black clouds through which only a single shaft of sunlight had penetrated. The images on the canvas revived sensations from the storm aboard the steamship a year before. Standing in the gallery on a hot August day in Philadelphia, she looked into the painting and felt again the crazy rolling of the ship beneath her feet and the sharp pricks of cold rain upon her face. She heard the roar of thunder coming closer and the shouting of crewmen. For a moment, she was *there* with the artist, at sea in the grip of the breaking storm.

Then a voice shattered her reverie. "Note how the artist has organized the painting in a triangular shape, with the sunlight forming one side of the triangle and the —"

"Do you ever just *look* at a painting, Mr. Faude?" Missy asked curtly.

"I beg your pardon?" the young man responded in surprise.

"I apologize for interrupting you," said Missy, for she did regret her poor manners. But she did not regret her question, and so she continued, "I meant to inquire if you ever simply look at a painting until you can feel it, without regard to issues of technique and history?"

Mr. Faude realized — he was a very smart man, after all — that Missy's seemingly simple question was in fact quite complicated.

"I believe that knowledge of such matters enhances one's pleasure in the work," he said rather pompously.

"But if the artist intended us to take pleasure in the mere arrangement of elements on the canvas, he could achieve his objective as well by painting only neat triangles and squares and circles," Missy observed.

Mr. Faude's smile and tone of voice were full of condescension as he said, "But my dear Miss Travilla, do you not see that this painting would not be half so appealing were it not for the geometric structure?"

"I understand that well, Mr. Faude," Missy replied, "but the structure is no more than a tool the artist employs to convey his meaning. In a good painting, as I believe this one to be, the tools and techniques of the artist should not be important if we understand his message. When you read a great book, Mr. Faude, do you judge it by the color of the ink or the quality of the paper?"

"I may refuse to read a badly printed book," he said, avoiding the real point of her question.

"And I may refuse to spend time with a badly painted picture," Missy said. "I have time for this painting because it speaks to my emotions and my experience first. Later I may concern myself with how it is painted and how the artist lived. But I must be inspired first."

"You make an interesting argument, Miss Travilla," Clarence Augustus conceded. "Is it not possible that we merely respond to art differently?"

"Yes, it is," replied Missy politely as they moved on to the next painting. She said no more on the subject, but she noted that Mr. Faude lectured about each new painting they saw, as if she had never expressed her opinion on the matter.

"Did you not think Miss Travilla very outspoken at the gallery today?" Mrs. Faude asked her son in the carriage as they returned to their hotel. They had taken Missy and Eddie home and enjoyed tea with the family before departing.

"Outspoken? I suppose one might say so," Clarence Augustus mused.

"I was quite taken aback," Mrs. Faude went on. "She is usually such a reserved young lady. But to question *you* about the merits of your knowledge of art!"

"I do not believe that was her intent, Mother," Mr. Faude said evenly. "In fact, the issue she raised is the subject of much debate among many students of the arts these days. Frankly, I was impressed by her spirit. I have wondered if Miss Travilla is not too reserved. But I see now that there is fire beneath her gentle façade."

"And you approve?" his mother asked in amazement.

"I approve of her spirit," Mr. Faude replied, "though as her husband, I would expect her to be subservient to me. But rest assured, Mother, I can teach her the correct manners of wife to husband. With some discipline, her spirit and intelligence can be cut and polished to the brilliance of a diamond."

"Then you plan to ask for her hand?" Mrs. Faude inquired hopefully.

"Oh, yes," he said. "I shall speak to her father at the first opportunity. Then I can begin her training in the proper role of a wife."

———

Missy did not know it, but her conversation with Mr. Faude had been overheard at the Academy that day. A young artist sat on a bench nearby, hidden behind the fronds of a large palm plant. Though unseen, he could clearly hear the words spoken. He listened closely — not from curiosity but because the voice of one of the speakers was so familiar to him — and he turned to view the scene.

He was tempted to rise and approach the little group. But when he observed the fine clothes and manners of Missy's two companions, he quickly gathered up his sketching book and pencils, rose from his seat, and rushed away in the opposite direction so that he would not be seen. Entering another room — his mind wholly on the beautiful face and figure of the girl who had occupied so many of his thoughts over the past year — he bumped into another patron of the arts who was inspecting a small, bronze sculpture.

The young artist lowered his head, muttered an apology, and was about to hurry on when a hearty voice stopped him.

"Lester Leland!"

So deeply caught was Lester in the vision of Missy Travilla that he failed at first to recognize her brother.

"It's I, Eddie Travilla. Golly, it's good to see you here. We've all wondered if you were still in Philadelphia, but no one knew how to get in touch with you."

By now, Eddie was pumping Lester's hand excitedly, and Lester could not help smiling into the boy's avid face.

"It's good to see you, Eddie. I hope your family is well."

"Very well, and they will all be so glad to know that I have encountered you. We're living not far from the Exhibition site for the summer. You've got to come and visit. How about tomorrow afternoon?"

Lester stammered the beginning of a refusal: "I don't think — I mean I doubt that —"

"I won't take no for an answer," Eddie laughed. "Mamma and Papa will be very angry with me if I let you go without making a firm date for an engagement. Tell me you can come tomorrow, for tea, about four o'clock."

"Well," Lester began hesitantly.

"Then it's settled," Eddie declared. "We're very casual, so don't dress up. In this heat, 'tea' means cold lemonade and root beer under the shade trees."

"Alright then, I'll be there," Lester agreed.

"That's great!" Eddie exclaimed, shaking Lester's hand again. "I wish we could talk now, but I must find Missy and rescue her from the fuddy-duddy who is our tour guide today. But we will see you tomorrow. Wait! Can I write on your pad?"

Lester handed over the pad and a pencil, and Eddie quickly wrote down the address of the Travillas' house.

"If you can't get a cab, there's a streetcar that stops just a block away," Eddie said, handing the sketchbook back. "Remember, four o'clock!"

What highs and lows of feeling Lester endured for the next twenty-four hours! The prospect of seeing and speaking with Missy again was sheer bliss to him. The knowledge that he was too poor to be more than a passing acquaintance plunged him into depression. Someday he would earn his reputation as a fine artist, but he could never ask a girl like Missy to wait until he made his name and fortune. To see Missy again had been his greatest desire. But now the prospect of seeing her was like torture. How could he bear to look upon the face and hear the sweet voice of the one he loved but could never approach?

By the next afternoon, Lester had definitely decided not to go to the Travillas'. As he polished his boots and brushed his jacket, he told himself that it was best for all concerned that he never see Missy or her family again. As he boarded the streetcar that took him to the Travillas' neighborhood, he determined to walk past their street and on to the Exhibition. As he rang the doorbell of the handsome house of his beloved, he thought that this afternoon must be his last view of her — a memory that he would hold in his heart forever.

The tea party was in full swing in the back garden. Horace and Rose Dinsmore were there, as well as the Travillas, and the family greeted Lester with all the warmth and affection of the proverbial father welcoming the prodigal son. Lester was engaged in excited conversation by one and all. They wanted to know what he had been doing, how his studies progressed, and would he return to Fairview in the fall.

"You owe us drawing lessons," Vi teased. "Doesn't he, Missy?"

A faint blush — which might have been from the heat — touched Missy's cheeks as she said, "I do not believe Mr. Leland 'owes' us anything, Vi. But I think we could learn a great deal from him, if he were able to instruct us."

"Draw something for us now, Mr. Leland. Please," begged Rosemary.

"Mr. Leland came here to relax," cautioned Missy. "He works very hard at drawing and painting, Rosemary, and you must not impose on him to work today."

But Rosemary's request had inspired Lester. He said that he would do quick sketches of all the Travilla children if they wished, and soon they were caught up in posing and watching over Lester's shoulder as he deftly captured each one in turn with his pencils. Even little Danny sat still for the few minutes it took to have his picture done. The twins posed together, then Rosemary, Vi, Eddie, and at last, Missy. Lester had often dreamed of painting her portrait, and now he lingered over the sketch, struggling to capture the brightness of her beautiful eyes, the perfect definition of her features, the softness of her complexion.

Lester could have happily sketched on for hours with Missy as his subject, but he was forced to stop when two maids appeared with trays of food and cool drinks. As the afternoon wound toward evening, Lester knew that he must depart. But Elsie and Edward would not let him go until he promised to make a return visit the following week. And Edward, escorting the young man to the door, renewed his offer that Lester tutor the Travilla daughters if he came to the South in the winter.

On the ride back to the city and in his small boarding-house room that night, Lester for once did not allow doubts and insecurities to trouble his thoughts. His happiness was, for the time, complete.

Another young man with his eye on the eldest daughter of the Travillas made an appearance at the house that very same night. It was Clarence Augustus Faude, who had requested a private appointment with Edward.

They met in the library at nine o'clock, and Mr. Faude presented his case. With Mr. Travilla's consent, Clarence Augustus would like to call on Miss Travilla with the intention of seeking an engagement to marry.

Edward listened attentively as Clarence Augustus enumerated all his many desirable qualifications as a potential husband. With great delicacy, the young man discussed his own financial position and his ability to manage Missy's inheritance to her advantage. Then Mr. Faude made an irredeemable error.

Lulled into speaking confidentially, he alluded in an offhanded manner to some youthful indiscretions during his travels. Saying that he had tired of such behavior quickly, Mr. Faude declared that he mentioned the matter only to assure Edward that he was a man of the world and unlikely ever to be tempted by tawdry pleasures in the future.

"Unlikely is not good enough," Edward said calmly.

"Sir?" Clarence Augustus said, his perfect composure failing him.

"It is one thing to be tempted," Edward replied, taking a tone that was not unkind but nonetheless admitted no argument. "But you have just told me that you have succumbed to temptation in the past. I realize that worldliness is supposed to be a virtue among men. But I regard the behavior of which you speak to be indicative of weakness."

"But you are a Christian," Clarence Augustus protested, "and surely we are obligated to forgive?"

"Forgive, yes, but not to ignore. You are asking to court my daughter with the object of marriage. I would be a poor father if, knowing that you have indulged yourself in the past, I put my daughter in jeopardy of future indiscretions. I do not sense that you are truly repentant, and so I advise you to turn back to the Word of God for guidance and to seek redemption from your Heavenly Father. In truth, Mr. Faude, you have a very high opinion of yourself for one so young. You also have a good mind and, I think, no intention to offend or do harm. Take my word for it; you must look deep inside yourself now. You are a child of God and no better than any other of His children. Approach Him with humility, and you will receive the forgiveness you need.

"But —"

"But there is no need to pursue your hopes with my daughter, for it is impossible. In any case, I believe that she

148

regards you as a friend and no more. You will probably think me cruel to be so direct, but you will realize eventually that I have saved you from a more painful rejection. You will be welcome here always, as a friend of the family, but I expect this conversation to put an end to any thoughts of a closer connection."

"I'm afraid I may have ended your friendship with Mrs. Faude," Edward said to Elsie as they prepared for bed that night.

"Be that as it may, you did what is right, dearest," Elsie said.

"I could have ended his hopes merely by saying that Missy is too young to consider marriage," Edward went on, "but I felt he needed to hear the truth. Clarence Augustus has many gifts and may become a worthy man if he can get past his conceit."

"And if he does, he will likely find an equally worthy wife," Elsie added. "His mother will be hurt and embarrassed by this, but she will mend. I can bear to lose her companionship if she and her son learn from the wisdom of your words," Elsie said. Then she put her hand to her husband's chin and looked into his eyes. "This is only the first of such conversations with would-be suitors that you will have, my darling," she said with a mischievous smile. "There are a number of young men, I think, who harbor thoughts of marrying our eldest child. And it will not be too many years before Vi is grown, then Rosemary —"

Edward's eyes twinkled in the way Elsie loved so, and he chuckled. "By the time Rosemary is eighteen, I shall be too ancient to show patience with ardent suitors. I will simply shake my wizened, old head and shout at them to be gone."

"To be serious, though, what if Missy herself comes to us with her own hopes of marrying?"

"She is young yet for marriage, but the ways of true love are never predictable. In truth, I am willing to trust her heart. We have always been honest and open with her, and she understands what marriage entails — the responsibilities as well as the pleasures. There is nothing of the flirt or fool about her. Yes, all in all, I am inclined to trust her feelings and her judgment, for I am confident she will choose well."

"This is the reward of parenting, isn't it, my love," Elsie said softly. "Our first child has reached adulthood, and we both have absolute confidence in her."

Recalling the closing words of the book of Second Peter, Edward said, "She has grown 'in the grace and knowledge of our Lord and Savior Jesus Christ.' We are her parents, but He will always be her guide and her protector."

CHAPTER

11

Matters of Love and Life

All my longings lie open before you, O LORD; my sighing is not hidden from you.

PSALM 38:9

$\mathcal{F}$or a number of very logical reasons, Lester Leland did travel to the South in November and take up residence with his aunt and uncle, Mary and John Leland, at Fairview. Lester had completed his studies with the master painter in Philadelphia. He wanted to begin a series of landscape paintings capturing the beauty and wildness of the South. He enjoyed the Southern climate and the company of his Southern family. He had the offer of work at Ion and felt sure he could find other families who wished their daughters and sons to have the advantage of drawing lessons. All very logical reasons — but the principle attraction of the South was one that Lester dared not admit fully to himself.

Lester was in love. His feelings for Missy were deep and true, yet he had no hope that he might ever declare his feelings and find them returned. He must content himself with being able to see his love, converse with her as tutor to pupil, and then retreat into the shadows. The pain of his situation was terrible, but the pain of not seeing Missy was more than he could endure.

The drawing lessons began in December. Two afternoons each week, Lester would ride from Fairview to Ion and spend an hour or so setting subjects for Missy and Vi to sketch and then guiding their work. Eddie, who was preparing himself to attend college the next year, sometimes joined the classes, though his interests differed greatly from his sisters'. Instead of still life drawings of cunningly arranged flowers and fruits, Eddie devoted his efforts to hard-edged renderings of architectural and engineering subjects. While Missy and Vi worked to learn the techniques for capturing the textures of natural objects in pencil, pastel, and water colors, Eddie concentrated on mathematically correct drawings in black-and-white of subjects ranging from individual tools found in the kitchen and workshop to the structure of Ion itself.

Lester proved to be an excellent teacher, though he had to struggle at times to keep his attention focused on the task at hand. He tended to be easily distracted by the way the winter sunlight through the drawing room windows sometimes caught the gold in Missy's brown hair or how a faint smudge of charcoal on her chin seemed to enhance her beauty. When he bent over her shoulder to correct a detail in her work, he could easily lose himself in the soft fragrance of her perfume. His students attributed these lapses of attention to the natural inclination of the artistic mind to daydream, though Vi soon noticed that her tutor's moments of absentmindedness usually happened when he was instructing her older sister.

As the winter wore on, Vi noticed something else odd. Missy, who had always been the most even-tempered of the Travilla children, would become moody at the strangest times. Though Missy displayed no change around others, Vi had several times come upon her sister sitting alone in her room, gazing out the window across the fields that separated Ion from Fairview, and smiling in that secret way that people have when they are deep in pleasurable thoughts. If Vi spoke, Missy didn't respond, as if she were caught in a trance.

Once Vi found Missy in the library, weeping silently. Thinking that something awful had happened, Vi rushed to embrace her sister and ask what was wrong.

"Oh, it's just that book," Missy sniffed as she pointed to a copy of *Jane Eyre* that lay open on the floor by her chair.

Vi picked up the book, smoothed its pages, and then eyed her sister carefully.

"You don't normally cry when you read novels," Vi observed.

"I do sometimes," Missy replied with uncharacteristic defensiveness, "when they are very sad. And it is so sad when Jane Eyre thinks she has lost all chance ever to marry the man she loves."

"But you know how the book ends," Vi said. "You have read it often enough."

Missy snatched the book from Vi's hand and retorted, "I know how many stories end, Vi, but I can still feel pity when I read them. Jane Eyre's terrible suffering nearly breaks my heart."

Feeling rejected, Vi turned and flounced across the room, stopping at the door to exclaim, "Well, at least Jane Eyre didn't sit around moping all the time and crying her eyes out over sentimental books!" Then she was gone before Missy could make a reply.

This little incident bothered Vi, for she hardly ever had cross words with her sister. She intended to apologize, but when she saw Missy an hour later, the elder girl was in merry spirits and seemed to have little recollection of the scene in the library.

"Oh, who cares about a book?" Missy laughed as she took Vi's arm. "We must hurry and get to the drawing room. Mr. Leland will be here soon, and I do so need his advice on that sketch I am working on."

Perplexed, Vi was nonetheless relieved at the return of her sister's good humor, and she decided to drop the matter. But Vi's curiosity was now aroused by her sister's erratic behavior, so she determined to watch closely. And Vi, who was nearing her thirteenth birthday and acutely aware of the emotions of others, was beginning to have strong suspicions about the cause of Missy's new unpredictability.

Spring arrived a little early that year, and as the weather warmed, all the Travillas welcomed the return of their outdoor activities. Visits to relatives and neighbors, horseback rides through field and forest, fishing in the local streams, games on the lawn, afternoon tea on the porch — the pace of the household picked up as the temperature climbed and the season burst into full blossom.

Missy adopted a new custom. Rising early each morning, she completed her Bible study and private devotion and hurried outdoors for a solitary walk before breakfast. Most days, she would take her sketchbook and wander down to the small lake — built by her father during the restoration of Ion after the war — which nestled serenely some distance from the house. The lake was fed by icy waters from an underground stream, and vegetation planted along the lake's shore was now thick and well tended. There was a narrow, grassy spot that Missy loved, near a cluster of willow trees that trailed their delicate limbs upon the water. A large bolder at the edge of the grassy plot offered seating. And if Missy arrived early enough, she could watch the steamy mist that rose off the lake's surface as the water was heated by the sun. Such times had an almost magical effect on her — as if she had been transported to the kind of fairytale place where all things were possible. Sometimes she would merely sit and look into the fog and let her imagination run freely. But more often, she would have conversations with her Heavenly

Friend, taking her troubles to Him and seeking His help and guidance.

One morning, she had tried to capture the diaphanous mist on the paper of her sketchbook but abandoned the attempt — thinking that she would have to ask Mr. Leland how to draw such a delicate cloud. Content with the beauty of her surroundings, she looked to the lake and listened to the sounds of morning. Water lapped gently at the grassy bank, a songbird made his music in a distant tree, a squirrel skittered through some dry leaves nearby. Then Missy became aware of the sound of splashing from the mist-shrouded lake. The noise was too loud to be a fish and had the rhythm of someone rowing the little boat kept for use on the lake.

The splashing seemed to come closer, and Missy got up from her seat on the rock and walked to the water's edge. A voice now accompanied the sound of the water. It was a high-pitched voice, like a child's, singing what Missy recognized as an old nursery tune. As she watched, a dark shape formed within the mist, moving in her direction. Missy had a worried thought that one of the servant's children may have taken the boat out without permission and become stranded on the water.

The dark shape resolved itself into the little boat, and Missy could see that someone was making jerky attempts to paddle it. She called out, "Hello," and the word reverberated across the water. The boat drifted closer, and Missy saw, to her horror, that its occupant was not a child but her Aunt Enna.

Enna — dressed in something white and with her hair rising all around her head like some bizarre feathered headdress — was sitting in the back of the small boat and lifting a wooden paddle in and out of the water in a comic parody of rowing. A large doll, which Missy knew to be her aunt's constant companion, sat propped up on the center seat of the boat. Enna was singing and humming scrapes of childhood songs and old hymns.

"Aunt Enna," Missy called out. "Can you row to the shore? Can you row this way?"

A sharp cackle rose from the boat, and Enna began to sing, "Row, row, row your boat. Row to the edge and over."

Suddenly, Enna dropped the paddle into the water and stood up. She snatched the doll from its seat and held it tightly to her cheek. In a screeching voice, the demented woman cried out, "Pretty dolly wants to swim! Swim over the edge!"

Enna started swaying from side to side, rocking the boat dangerously. All the while, she continued to cackle and scream: "Over the edge! Over the edge! Pretty dolly wants to swim!"

If I had some rope, Missy thought, looking around desperately and seeing nothing with which to effect a rescue. She knew that the lake was deepest at this spot, eight or ten feet at least. Could Aunt Enna swim? Missy didn't know. Perhaps her aunt's screams would bring help, but she couldn't wait to find out. The boat was rocking wildly now, and Missy yelled, "Sit down, Aunt Enna! Sit down now! Dolly wants to sit down!"

Enna stopped swaying, and for an instant Missy thought her aunt would do as commanded. But the boat was still rocking, and Enna lost her balance. If she had dropped the doll, she might have righted herself. But she hugged the toy, and in an image that would never leave Missy, Enna seemed to fly over the edge of the boat like a white bird. She hit the water and disappeared.

Without another thought, Missy kicked off her slippers and plunged into the lake. Her light calico dress and petticoat ballooned around her and buoyed her briefly. The boat was not far from shore, and Missy kept her eyes riveted to the point where Enna had disappeared. Missy was a strong swimmer, and she reached the spot quickly. Her clothes, now soaked, pulled at her like a weight of iron, but she kept her head and looked around her.

A hand emerged from the lake, and Missy grasped it, pulling upward as she kicked furiously to stay above water. A head appeared, and with a mighty effort, Missy grabbed her aunt's hair. She got her arm over Enna's shoulder and across her chest. With her other arm, she stroked, literally pulling at the water and forcing her way forward. She kicked and stroked furiously, holding her aunt above the water. Water filled Missy's mouth, and she spat and coughed to get her breath.

One thought ran over and over in her head: "God, help me." Never once did it occur to her to loosen her hold on Enna and save herself.

She stroked and kicked, stroked and kicked, but her progress was agonizingly slow and her strength faded rapidly in the cold water. She felt herself sinking and fought to get her head above the water. Gasping for air, she sank again. But still she held onto Enna.

Missy knew that she was about to lose consciousness, but she reached forward in the water once again, putting all that remained of her strength into the movement, and she felt something take hold of her arm.

From somewhere near her, a voice shouted, "Hang on, Missy!"

Her arm was held in a vise-like grip, and she felt herself being dragged. She raised her head and gulped air. Her eyes closed, she breathed again, and she clung on to her aunt.

In another minute, strong arms were lifting Missy, Enna, and their rescuer onto the grassy bank. Missy was rolled onto her stomach and firm hands pressed against her back, forcing the water from her lungs. She sputtered and coughed, and felt the rush of pure air that filled her. She was gently turned over again and grasped in an embrace. She was lifted by more strong arms, and just before everything went black, she heard her father's voice. "Thank you, dear God. Thank you."

The next few days were filled with anxious prayer. Missy would recover, Dr. Barton declared, but she had been greatly weakened by the experience and must be confined to bed until she regained her strength. She slept for nearly twenty-four hours after being pulled from the lake. When she awoke, she seemed to have no idea where she was, causing both Elsie and Edward several minutes of fearful concern. Then, Missy's mind cleared. She smiled at her parents and said, "You saved me, Papa. I felt your hand on my arm, and I knew I was saved. And then I heard you thanking God."

"Thank God I did, child," Edward replied, "then and a thousand times more over the last day and night. But it was not my hand that saved you."

Missy was confused. "But it had to be you, Papa. I felt your hand and heard you tell me to hang on. And you said something else, but I could not understand your words. And then I was pulled onto the bank."

"I lifted you to the bank and carried you back to the house, but it was Mr. Leland who saved you in the water."

"You and your Aunt Enna," Elsie added, her eyes moist with tears of joy. "I don't know how Mr. Leland came to be in that place. I only know that God led him. Just as God brought you there to meet your aunt's need."

"Aunt Enna is alive, then?" Missy asked.

"She is, though her condition is grave," Edward said. "We believe that when she fell from the boat, she struck her head on the wooden paddle that was floating on the water. She is still unconscious, and Dr. Barton cannot say what damage she may have suffered until she wakes. But she is alive, thanks to you, my brave daughter, and to Mr. Leland."

Missy raised herself on her arm and asked urgently, "Is he here, Papa? Is Mr. Leland here? I must tell him of my gratitude."

"No, he insisted on returning to Fairview," Edward answered. "Lie down now, Missy, and rest. The doctor says you need sleep and nourishment, and if you follow his instructions, you should be back to your old self within a week."

"But is Mr. Leland well, Papa?" Missy wanted to know.

"He is fine, dear," Edward assured.

"Ben took Mr. Leland to Fairview and stayed with him for several hours yesterday. And your Cousin Art paid a visit there while Dr. Barton was tending to you and Enna," Elsie explained. "Art reports that Mr. Leland is dry and fit and that Mary Leland is feeding him on her pot roast and apple pie. Art assured Mr. Leland that his star pupil was also doing well. I imagine that Mr. Leland will pay you a visit as soon as he thinks you are up to it."

Missy flushed and lay back upon her pillow. "You understand my interest, don't you, Mamma?" she said with a soft sigh. "I really must be able to thank him. I really must."

Elsie was tucking the covers around her daughter. "I understand, dearest. And I am sure we will see Mr. Leland quite soon. But you must rest now. I will sit with you, and Aunt Chloe will be here shortly with soup and tea."

"And I will come back later and read to you," Edward promised. "I see that you have another Charlotte Bronte novel at your bedside."

Missy smiled at her parents and thanked them once more. Then she closed her eyes, but she didn't sleep. All she could think of was Lester Leland's hand on her arm, pulling her to safety — saving her from a watery death — and saying something to her that, as hard as she tried, she could not remember.

At Fairview, Mary Leland was indeed feeding her favorite nephew on beef and apple pie — and anything else he might want. The whole Leland family treated Lester as a hero, and if he had been a different sort of man, Lester could have taken great advantage of the situation.

In fact, the attention and the compliments caused him more pain than pride. When others praised him for his quick thinking and action, their remarks simply reminded him of Missy. He was always sure to point out her bravery, making it clear to everyone that Mrs. Enna Johnson would be dead except for Missy's courage and selfishness. Otherwise he avoided talk of the rescue and of the Travillas in general.

Mary Leland began to wonder at Lester's strange reaction when he came up with one reason after another not to visit Ion, though several invitations had come from Mrs.

Travilla. Then Lester excused himself from further tutoring. He wrote to Edward Travilla, explaining that his painting master in Philadelphia had urged Lester to apply for an artist's stipend that would enable him to study in Italy. The process was complicated, Lester wrote, and he would need all his time to prepare a portfolio of works to submit to the application committee. (This was, in the main, true, though Lester had almost completed his letter of application and his portfolio was already nearly done.) He explained all this to his aunt and uncle as well — then asked to take on more work on the plantation for pay that was far less than he received as a drawing tutor. When Mary questioned her nephew about this decision, he said that he preferred farm labor to teaching and the exercise would help him build up his strength.

It was when Mary realized that Lester had not finished a new drawing or painting in several weeks and that his painting box was gathering dust in his bedroom that she decided to speak plainly.

One night when the rest of the family was abed, Mary saw that the light still burned in Lester's room. She went to his door and knocked. He bid her to enter, and when she did, she saw that he was hurriedly putting what appeared to be a drawing into a drawer of his chest.

He turned to her with that sheepish look she always thought so appealing, and he said, "Yes, Aunt Mary?"

With the determination that has served mothers since the beginning, Mary Leland said crisply, "Sit down, Lester. We must have a talk now."

CHAPTER

12

Love, Hope, and Questions

Strengthen me with raisins,
refresh me with apples, for
I am faint with love.

Song of Songs 2:5

*N*ephew, the time has come for you to tell me what is going on," Mrs. Leland continued. "I am neither your mother nor father, but I have an obligation to them, and a responsibility to you. Let's sit down, my dear."

Lester, who was unprepared for but not really surprised by his aunt's visit, took a seat on the straight-backed chair at his desk while Mary Leland settled into a more comfortable easy chair. Lester looked at his aunt but said nothing.

"You're an adult, Lester, and you don't have to tell me anything you don't want to," Mary went on in a kindly tone. "But I'm concerned for you, and I want to help if I can. Since the accident at Ion, I have seen changes in you that I don't understand. You refuse Mrs. Travilla's invitations. You have given up tutoring, an occupation that you clearly enjoyed. And most telling, you have all but stopped painting. Until a month ago, you would show me sketches almost every day for your Southern landscapes. When you cease doing the work that you love, I know that something is wrong."

Mary leaned forward in her chair. Her face softened as she added, "I love you, Nephew, as do your uncle and all your family here. To see you in pain — well, pain is sometimes easier to bear when we talk of it with someone who cares about us."

"I am truly sorry if I have caused you to worry, Aunt Mary," Lester said at last. "Since there is little that can be done about my situation, I didn't want to burden you with my troubles."

"Does our Heavenly Father turn away when you take your problems to Him?"

"Never," Lester said firmly.

"Well, I have taken my worries to Him, and I believe that He has guided me to speak with you."

"But there is nothing you can do for me," he said, bowing his head and twisting his strong, well-shaped hands in his lap.

"Forgive my directness, but are you in love with Missy Travilla?"

Lester gaped at his aunt. Now she had surprised him, and he blurted out, "How did you know?"

Mary smiled gently. "I am not blind to the longings of the heart," she said. "I have observed little things, Lester — the tone of your voice when you mention her name, the lightness of your step whenever you left here to visit Ion for a lesson."

"It's true," the young man said. "I guess that I have loved her since I first saw her aboard that steamer."

"She is a beautiful young woman."

A rapturous smile came to Lester's face. "More beautiful than any other," he said, "but it is a beauty far deeper than her physical appearance. I have tried to do a portrait of her, but how does one capture such loveliness of spirit with brush and paint?"

"And have you told her of your feelings?"

Lester flushed. "One time," he said. "It was when we were in the lake. I had seized her arm. I told her to hang on, and then without thinking, I said 'I love you.' No one heard me, least of all Missy, for she was barely conscious."

"Then you must speak more plainly to her."

"How can I? She is a young woman of lofty social position and wealth. I am a poor painter. Even if she returned my affection, what could I offer her? She has many suitors,

Aunt Mary. I have seen them. Sophisticated men of high birth and money. They can give her anything she wants. I cannot compete."

"Perhaps she does not expect you to offer anything beyond your true love. Missy has never struck me as the kind of girl who cares much for material possessions."

"Perhaps she doesn't, but what of her family? I do not imagine that they would welcome the attentions of a struggling artist."

"You may have imagined what is not true. The Travillas are as openhearted a family as I have ever met. They live in the ways of our Lord, Lester, every day and in every way. Have I ever told you what they did for us?"

Lester, who knew only that his aunt and uncle were close friends of the Travillas, looked at his aunt questioningly.

Mary settled back into her chair. "When we first came to Fairview just after the war, we were not welcomed in this area. The South had endured so much loss, and we were Northerners — 'Yankees' and 'carpetbaggers' to most of our neighbors. Even at church, people would turn their backs on us, and I must tell you that we seriously considered abandoning this place and returning to the North. But then we met the Travillas, and they instantly opened their home and hearts to us. Through them we came to know Horace and Rose Dinsmore and their friendship. They felt no prejudice or no need to placate the neighbors' ill will toward us. And by their example, they led others to accept us. I have known the Travillas and Dinsmore for ten years now, and there is not a drop of snobbery in any of them."

"I believe you, but still —"

"Oh, Lester, what have you to lose if you speak to Mr. and Mrs. Travilla?" Mary declared. "Should they refuse your request to address their daughter, will you be in any worse a situation than you are now? But if you do not speak your heart and mind, will you not always regret that you never made the effort? To me, the latter is by far the more terrible torment."

"But even if they agreed, Aunt Mary, I could not marry for at least another year or two and maybe even longer. I believe that I may well receive the stipend to study in Italy, for my old teacher is very confident. What then? How could I ask Missy to wait for my return? She is nineteen now, the age for merriment and parties. It would be like asking her to sacrifice the best years of her youth."

"Nonsense!" Mary laughed. "You men have all too little faith in the resilience of women. If she loves you as you love her, she will wait with joy."

"Do you really think there is hope for me?" Lester asked, his eyes shining with a brightness his aunt hadn't seen in weeks.

"Of course, there is hope. There is always hope. But nothing will happen if you hide away here and continue to make yourself miserable. I remember a line from a poem by Robert Burns that will serve you well — 'And let us mind, faint heart ne'er won a lady fair.' Be bold of heart, and there is hope you may win your heart's desire. You showed great courage when you went into the lake to save Missy and her aunt. Summon up that courage again, dear Nephew."

Lester and his aunt talked on into the night, until he had decided on his course of action. Then she kissed him on the brow, reminded him to say his prayers, and bade him a good night. It was quite late when Lester finally was ready for sleep, however. A letter now lay on his desk, ready for delivery the next day. And his prayers were somewhat lengthy. Just before going to his bed, he opened his chest drawer to look once more at the drawing he kept there — the sweet face of his beloved as he had first sketched her in the garden of the Travillas' summer house in Philadelphia.

"Well, Lester, we thought we might never see you again," Edward said jovially as he ushered the young man into the library at Ion the next evening. "I was delighted to get your note asking to see us tonight."

"We have never thanked you properly for saving our precious daughter and my aunt," Elsie added, extending her hand to her guest.

"No thanks are necessary, Mrs. Travilla, for I merely did what you both would have done in my place," Lester replied shyly.

"But we were not in your place," Edward said, "and I cannot bear to think what might have happened had you not come along. Accept our gratitude, Lester, and know that we thank God daily for your bravery and quick thinking."

"I believe Mr. Leland has come to speak with us on other business tonight," Elsie commented. "Come, sit by the fire, and tell us what is on your mind."

Lester took the offered seat and began — hesitantly at first, but with growing confidence when he saw that the Travillas listened to his words with the utmost respect and seriousness.

He spoke plainly and from the heart, telling the parents of his love for their daughter and his hope that he might be permitted to speak to Miss Travilla on the subject of marriage. He talked of his prospects, honestly stating that the fortunes of an artist were rarely so easy to predict as those of a businessman. Then he told them about the possibility of his study in Italy and his expected absence of a year or more.

"I realize that I am not yet in a position to support her financially, but I will do everything in my power to be worthy of her, if she is willing to wait for me."

Edward cast a sideways glance at his wife, measuring her thoughts; then he turned back to Lester and said, "I appreciate your straightforward speech, Lester. Others have come to me with the same request, but none have been so forthright as you, and I have turned them away without hesitation. You must understand that my children are the jewels in my crown, and I will not hand them over easily."

Elsie saw a momentary look of desperation flash in Lester's eyes. To her husband, she said gently, "Do not prolong Mr. Leland's agony, dearest."

Edward's countenance relaxed into a wide smile as he went on, "Lester, I can think of no gentleman I would like more for a son-in-law, but the answer you seek is neither mine nor my wife's to give. You have our blessings so long as the young lady we all love is in agreement."

Hearing these words, Lester dropped his head briefly, letting out the deep breath he had been holding. Then he looked up again and asked, "When may I speak to her, sir?"

"Is there a better time than now?" Edward said.

Elsie rose from her chair, saying, "I believe Missy is in the sitting room. It would be my pleasure to summon her here. And then perhaps you might enjoy a walk along the veranda to the garden. The moon is near full tonight, and its light may favor romance."

Before leaving the room, Elsie stepped close to Lester and kissed him quickly on the cheek. "I wish you well in your quest," she whispered.

Elsie and Edward remained in the library while Missy and Lester retired to stroll in the spring garden.

The parents tried to read, which had been their original plan for the evening. But neither could focus on the words in their books. After a few minutes, Elsie moved from her chair to sit beside her husband on the couch. Edward wrapped his arm around her shoulder, nestling her in the crook of his arm. She lay her head against his shoulder.

"What do you think she will say?" Edward asked.

"If her behavior of late is any indication, I believe her answer will be pleasing to Mr. Leland," Elsie replied.

Indeed, Missy had not been her usual self since the incident at the lake. Her parents had feared at first that she suffered some undiagnosed physical after-effect, but both Dr. Barton and Art Conley had assured them otherwise. Yet each day that passed, Missy had become more pale and nervous. When they learned that Mr. Leland was canceling the drawing classes, Missy reacted with an outburst of crying that was totally out of character for her. Everyone in the household had grown worried about her, none more so than Elsie and Edward.

It was Aunt Chloe who divined the true nature of the problem. She and Elsie were cleaning up the toys in the nursery one day after the children had gone outside to play, and Elsie raised the subject of Missy.

"If we see no improvement soon, Edward and I have agreed that we will take her to a specialist in Philadelphia. I fear that her health is in danger."

Chloe laughed, and Elsie looked at her old nursemaid in shock.

Elsie's Great Hope

"No doctor can cure what ails that girl," Chloe chuckled.

"What do you mean?" Elsie asked.

"Well, Miss Elsie, I do believe our Missy has a sickness no specialist can help. She's sick with love. I've seen it too many times to miss the symptoms. Can't eat. Can't concentrate. Cries at the drop of a hat and walks around this house like a ghost. It's love, Miss Elsie, that's troublin' that girl's heart."

"Love!" exclaimed Elsie. "Love for whom?"

"Why, I can't say for absolute sure," Chloe continued, "but it seems to me the trouble started when Mr. Lester didn't come back here to see her after the accident. She was doin' right well after a couple of days in bed, then you remember how he sent his regrets to that first invitation of yours?"

"I do."

"That's when I noticed Missy hangin' around the house and starin' out the front windows like she was expectin' someone to ride up the driveway any minute. She sank a little lower each day, and you know how she nearly cried her eyes out when he wrote that he wouldn't be givin' any more drawin' lessons."

The truth of Chloe's observations struck Elsie. "I thought she was just upset about not having the lessons. But why didn't I see these things?" she asked.

" 'Cause you and Mr. Edward have been worried about the health of her body, just like good parents should be. But I looked at Missy, and I remembered another lovesick young girl who moped and cried and tried to hide her misery when she thought her man was goin' to marry someone else. That young girl was you, Miss Elsie, and Missy has always been the image of her mama."

"Oh, dear," Elsie sighed, "what can I do to help her?"

"Nothin' except to give her all your love and support. I wouldn't say anythin' to her yet. Give her some time to work it out for herself."

"And why do you think Mr. Leland has been so distant?"

"Well, I guess that boy's probably in his own kind of misery. If he loves Missy, which I suspect he does, he's got to be thinkin' about how poor he is and how he can never give her all the things she has now. He probably knows in his heart that she doesn't care a bit about fancy finery, but he's got pride, you know. He doesn't want to appear to be like some of those fortune-hunting types who thought they could steal our Missy away."

"Those poor children," Elsie sighed.

"Love's not easy between men and women," Chloe said, placing a warm hand on Elsie's shoulder, "but if it's true love, those two young folks will find a way to make it work. Question for you is this, Miss Elsie. Would you and Mr. Edward want Mr. Leland for a son?"

Elsie contemplated for a minute. Then she said, "Yes, Aunt Chloe, I would be proud to have him as a son. He's a fine Christian man with a good heart and a gentle spirit. If he truly loves Missy and she loves him, I believe it would be a lasting love. That is what I want for her — and all the children. Love that can endure the hardships as well as the happiness of marriage."

"Then you just pray hard for those two. That's what I've been doin'," Chloe advised. "If the good Lord wants them to be together, He'll show them the way."

Elsie's Great Hope

The younger children were snug in the beds; Eddie, Vi, and the twins had repaired to their rooms for their nightly devotions and to await their parents' good night.

The fire had died down in the fireplace, but since it was a warm night, Edward had not added more fuel. He and Elsie knew they must go to the other children soon, but they could not bring themselves to leave the library. The house had become very quiet, and only the steady ticking of the clock on the mantel broke the silence. The oil lamp was burning low, and shadows grew in the corner of the room. Still the parents did not rise from the couch.

Then came a soft knock at the door, and Missy's voice called out, "Are you still there, Mamma? Papa?"

"We're here, darling," Elsie answered. "Come in."

The door opened and in the light from the hall, Elsie and Edward saw the silhouetted figures of their daughter and Mr. Leland.

"We have news for you," Missy said. "The most wonderful news in the world!"

CHAPTER

13

A Family Gathering

*"I will make you into a great nation
and I will bless you; I will make
your name great, and you will
be a blessing.*

GENESIS 12:2

A Family Gathering

From Molly's journal, dated July 4, 1877:

It is almost midnight, and I should be asleep, but the events of the evening have inspired me to open my journal and record my observations. Tonight we marked the end of a full year of celebration of the birth of our nation at a large gathering at The Oaks. Everyone was there — all the families of Ion and Roselands and Tinegrove. The Carringtons came, too. And the Lelands, of course. Rosie, her husband, and their new baby arrived from The Laurels. And everyone was happy to see Trip and his lovely wife. They, too, are parents now, and the newest Horace Dinsmore is an energetic, outgoing toddler who clearly delights his grandparents and great-grandfather with his happy personality.

For the first time in too many years, my own family was reunited: Dick — now Dr. Percival — and Bob and Betty, who continue to thrive in Uncle Horace and Aunt Rose's care, and I. But the real miracle is our Mamma. After the accident at the lake last spring, I thought that she would be taken from us. She did not recover consciousness for more than three weeks, and when she did open her eyes, she was unable to speak for many days. How sad she was — like a frail child lying upon her bed and gazing at us as if she had never seen us before. But as her strength returned, her memory improved, and she began to talk again. The effects of the blow she received when she fell from the rowboat are now clear. She will never have the mental abilities of an adult, but she is no longer the spoiled and willful child she became after her first accident. She is childish still, but sweet in temper and gentle in spirit. She remembers me now, and Dick, Betty, and Bob. She lives at Ion, and although she has a nurse, Mamma often sits with me while I am working. We walk in the gardens every day, and she takes great pride in pushing my chair. At night, I brush her long hair, and we sing hymns together. It is strange the way we humans can adapt, for Mamma and I have found a peace that we never had before her tragedies. And I thank God each day for giving me this opportunity to honor and serve her.

(I see that I have digressed. The point of this writing is to tell about the party.)

We arrived at The Oaks in the afternoon to see the flag of our country raised on a pole newly installed in front of the house. It was a brilliant sight as it fluttered against the backdrop of clear, blue sky. We then gathered on the side lawn, where long tables were laid with great platters and serving dishes. Hams and fried chicken, vegetables and fruits from the garden, fresh baked breads, and a bounty of desserts including my favorite — Mrs. Leland's apple pie. Tables and chairs were arranged about the lawn for the adults, and the children picnicked on blankets. It was just what Aunt Rose wanted, an all-American feast fit for our nation's birthday.

After our meal, the chairs were moved into a large semi-circle, and Uncle Horace instructed the servants to fill everyone's glass with lemonade. Then Uncle asked the servants to take glasses for themselves and to join our circle.

"We are now at the opening of a second century of our democracy, facing a future of great promises and enormous challenges," he said. "Who in 1776 could have dreamed that from the seeds of their revolution, a strong and proud nation would grow? Our United States now span the continent from Atlantic to Pacific and are home for more than forty million people who have come here from all corners of the world to seek freedom and opportunity. We have endured much suffering on the journey to this point, and we have become a better and stronger people. Yet much remains to be done if all our citizens are to share in the fruits of our freedom. Those of us who have lived through so much of our nation's history must teach what we have learned to our next generations. The lessons of the past cannot be forgotten. As we read in the book of Romans, 'For everything that was written in the past was written to teach us, so that through endurance and the encouragement of the Scriptures we might have hope.'"

Then Uncle raised his glass in tribute to "all the brave and honorable men and women whose sacrifices have brought us to this day of celebration."

When everyone had drunk the lemonade, Uncle Horace resumed by asking God's blessing upon the nation and praying for the guidance of our Heavenly Father in our second century. He concluded with words that brought tears to many eyes. "Help us, dear Father, to heal the wounds of war and oppression, but never to forget the cause of our sorrows. Help us to remember the words of the Declaration of Independence, 'that all men are created equal.' Teach us to be just to one another and to demand justice for all. Teach us to rejoice in our differences and to treat one another as we wish to be treated. Be with us, Father — 'our refuge and strength, an ever-present help in trouble' — as we remember the past and build the future. Amen."

Uncle Horace then asked Cousin Edward to come forward.

"We may need more lemonade," Edward began, "for I, too, wish to propose a toast."

His announcement did not come as a surprise to anyone, but we all joined in the pleasure of the moment as if we were being taken unawares.

Edward opened with some jesting remarks about his own age, and then he paid gallant compliments to Cousin Elsie. Coming to his real purpose, he spoke briefly of the joys of fatherhood. It was a witty and charming speech that ended with the announcement of the engagement of Missy and Lester Leland and a toast to the couple. There was much clapping and a few cheers raised by the younger children. We all gathered round the happy pair to offer congratulations and hear about their plans.

Lester has been awarded a generous study stipend, and he would be leaving the country for Europe in September. Missy and I have talked several times of the difficulties of a long separation from her beloved, and she is working very hard to accept the necessary wait. She told me something that I had not heard before — that Uncle Horace made Elsie and Edward wait for a full year between their engagement and marriage. "I guess it has become a family custom," Missy said with good humor. "If long engagements produce the kind of marriage my parents have, then I am satisfied to wait."

I think there was a bit of false bravery in her remark. Her parents, after all, weren't separated during their engagement. Missy and Lester will not even see one another for a year. But I am a romantic, and I have every confidence in the strength of their love for one another.

(It must be the late hour, but I have strayed from my purpose again. I shall never be a great writer if I cannot learn to stay firmly on course!)

After the announcement, everyone mingled and chatted for a very pleasant hour. The sun set brilliantly. The side lawn at The Oaks stretches downward to a wide, shallow plain of planted fields, and beyond this fertile plain rises a low line of wooded hills. As the sun dropped to just above the crest of the hills, the whole sky seemed to explode in color—the sun itself a great ball of crimson. Lester said that it was as if God had chosen a palette of the richest reds, blues, and golds to mark the country's celebration. We all simply sat in awe as we watched the sun complete its daily journey. As the sun's setting light faded, stars seemed to pop out in the sky — glittering little specks of light that brightened as the night deepened.

Lanterns were quickly lit around the lawn and garden, and most of the guests assumed that the party was drawing to a close. But Uncle Horace had a surprise in store for us. Mamma and I were chatting with Cousin Isa when a sharp whistling sound cut through our words, and a bright display like a shower of white stars exploded high above us.

Then more fireworks were launched from a spot at the far edge of the lawn. For ten minutes at least, we were rapt by the pyrotechnics. The night sky seemed to bloom into a garden of gigantic red, white, and blue blossoms, and each new burst brought a fresh chorus of oohs and ahs from the guests. A final explosion of at least five or six of the fireworks seemed to bring the show to an end. But Uncle had one more surprise for us.

Our attention was drawn to a point beyond a low hedge some twenty or thirty yards away. Lights flared and before our eyes appeared a blazing image of our grand old flag. The fireworks flag seemed almost to wave with light, and I found myself joining everyone in happy shouts of "Hoorah! Hoorah!" It was a spectacle that seemed to me to rival any I had seen at the Philadelphia Centennial.

That was not the last of my surprises, however. Most of the guests departed soon after, but we stayed on for a while. Elsie and Missy disappeared into the house with Aunt Rose, while Bob and Betty escorted Edward and Lester on a tour of the rose garden, which had been gaily illuminated by hanging, colored, paper lanterns.

I remained with Mamma at a table on the lawn, for she had fallen into a sweet sleep and I did not want to disturb her until we were ready to leave. Uncle Horace joined us there, taking a chair beside mine. In low voices, we talked. I told him what a glorious evening it had been, complimenting the fireworks. But I said that I had particularly appreciated his remarks earlier in the night. I said something about the importance of history and how

I believed that the nation's history was really the collected histories of all the families of the land.

"It is interesting you say that," Horace answered, "for I have been thinking much about my family lately. I am now one of the elders of our tribe, you know."

"An elder," I laughed, "but hardly elderly, Uncle Horace. You wear each of your years with grace."

"But I am not proud of all my years," he said. "There's a part of my family who might have been here with us tonight, were it not for an act of neglect on my part. Have you ever heard of the Stanhopes, Molly?"

"Of Aunt Wealthy Stanhope," I replied. "I've heard many wonderful stories about her. She is your mother's sister, I believe."

"Half-sister. My mother, Eva, and Wealthy had the same father, but my mother and her sister, Eleanor, were the daughters of his second marriage. And Eleanor had a daughter named Marcia, who was a dear friend of my childhood and youth. But the last time I saw her was before I departed for Europe, just after I completed my university studies. That was some forty years ago."

At that moment, Elsie walked up. She put her hand on her father's shoulder and asked, "What was forty years ago, Papa? Are you being nostalgic tonight?"

"I was telling Molly about the Stanhopes, dear," he said as he rose and brought another chair to our small circle. Elsie took her seat, and Uncle resumed his.

Elsie's Great Hope

"I was speaking of the Stanhopes and of a cousin I have not seen for many years. Her name is Marcia Keith, the daughter of my mother's sister, Eleanor."

"Marcia Keith? I've heard that name, Papa," Elsie said. "Could Aunt Wealthy have mentioned her?"

"That is quite likely," Horace replied. "Marcia lived with Aunt Wealthy for many years — long before Harry Duncan did."

"Do you correspond with your cousin Marcia?" I asked.

"She tried to maintain contact with me, for a number of years. Marcia and her husband and children were fine people and true Christians. When I last visited them, I told them the story of my marriage to Elsie's mother and of my daughter's birth. They did all they could to help me and encourage me to reclaim my child, but I was an arrogant young man at that time, self-involved and certain I needed no one's advice or support to make my own decisions. I appreciated their prayers on my behalf, but my grief and misery were so intense that I could never bring myself to answer Marcia's letters. I suppose she gave up or assumed that her letters did not reach me. I was a very selfish man, Molly, before I found the love of our Lord Jesus."

I tried to protest, for Uncle Horace has always been in my eyes the most generous of men.

"I am honest about my youthful follies," he said. Although I could not see his face clearly, I heard the wistfulness in my dear uncle's voice as he went on, "When I opened my heart to God, He opened my eyes to many things about myself, both good and unpleasant."

"Then you have not heard from Marcia in all these years?" Elsie inquired.

"No, nor any of her children. And I would like to know what has happened to them. They are my family, and family to you, Elsie, and to Trip and Rosie. Yet through my neglect, I have cut off that part of our history from my children and grandchildren."

"I would like to meet them, Papa," Elsie said.

"In fact you have, dear," he said, "just after you, Mrs. Murray, and Aunt Chloe went to live at Roselands. But you were very young and do not remember them."

"Surely you can trace them, Uncle Horace," I said. "Your Aunt Wealthy must know where they are."

"I am sure she does, but I think it may be too late. I was not there for them for so many years. They would be right to resent and reject my intrusion upon them now."

At this remark, I gathered my courage and said, "They are just as likely to welcome you, Uncle Horace, and your family. You said that they are good Christians. Is it not unjust to discredit them when you have no idea how they will react? Please forgive my frankness, Uncle, but I have been told how you once assumed you knew someone else's motives and nearly lost the love of your precious daughter as a result. You spoke so eloquently tonight of how we must learn from the lessons of the past. I have not nearly the experience of life that you have, but I have learned this — we must sometimes risk rejection if we are ever to reap rewards."

I held my breath, hoping I had not said too much. Then I felt his hand cover mine, and he said, "You have wisdom beyond your years, Molly. And you are right. The separation from my Stanhope relatives is of my making, and I am the one who must bridge the gap. I shall write to them and ask their forgiveness. It will not be an easy letter, for you know our Dinsmore pride."

I had to laugh then, for no one is better acquainted with the Dinsmore pride than I am.

"I wish I possessed your gift with words," Uncle said. "I have a verse of Scripture that always runs through my head when I think of your talent, as I often do. It is from the book of Isaiah: 'Go now, write it on a tablet for them, inscribe it on a scroll, that for the days to come it may be an everlasting witness.'"

"And I have a phrase from the Scriptures that may help you as you compose your letter," I responded. "'Write them on the tablet of your heart.' Open your heart and the words will come. Oh, Uncle, is it rude for me to ask that you tell me the outcome of your effort? I am terribly curious, which is a virtue in my chosen profession but often ill-mannered in other circumstances."

"Of course, I shall inform you," he said. "Let us hope my letter will reap the rewards you spoke of."

"It will, Papa," Elsie said. "I shall pray for you and our cousins and for our reunion. Molly and I will both pray, won't we?"

I agreed enthusiastically, for I wanted nothing more than my dear Uncle's happiness.

At that moment, Mamma began to stir from her catnap, and we turned our attention to her. But even as we took our leave and made the carriage ride home, I could not stop thinking about Uncle's story and the family he has lost and now hopes to find. I will certainly pray for him, that our Lord gives Uncle the courage to pursue his quest and rebuild his connection to his loved ones.

It is astonishing how the bonds of family may be both tight and elastic; they hold us together through the worst of times, yet they easily expand to include each new member. The circle of our family enlarged tonight with the addition of Lester and the Lelands. Perhaps there will be more additions when next we gather together. If Uncle Horace is successful in his efforts to reunite with the Keiths, there may be many new stories to tell!

But what could have caused Uncle Horace to cut off all contact with these members of his family? He blamed himself for the estrangement, but he really didn't explain. He said that Elsie had met her relatives when she was little. What might they know of her early life? I realize that my cousin's mind is on other things right now, but she must be a little curious. I certainly am. Oh dear, I am being nosey, but I cannot help wondering what secrets will be revealed if we ever meet the Keiths.

CHAPTER 14

The Hope of the Future

Tell it to your children, and let your children tell it to their children, and their children to the next generation.

JOEL 1:3

The Hope of the Future

s Molly was writing away in her journal that night, Elsie and Edward were together on the small porch outside their bedroom. The sky seemed awash in stars, and a soft night breeze blew away some of the heat that always lingers in July.

The Travillas sat side by side in comfortable chairs, their hands linked.

"I do not feel old enough to be the father of the bride," Edward said.

"I do not feel quite ready to part with our firstborn," Elsie replied. "It seems only yesterday that I first held her in my arms. Remember how lovely an infant she was? And now she is a grown woman who will soon be leaving us, though we have a year with her yet."

"But she is not leaving us," Edward said. "None of our children will ever leave us, no matter how far away they are. Look at the stars, dearest. Think of how distant they are. Millions—no, billions of miles away. Yet they return their light to us each night. Our children are like the stars."

"I always think of Lily when I look at the stars," Elsie said softly. "She is beyond even them, yet she is also in my heart, and someday we will be with her again."

"No parting was ever harder than that one, but we survived it because we have our Lord's promise of eternal reunion. Elsie love, are you truly saddened by Missy's engagement?"

"Oh, not at all. I see how deeply she loves Lester and he loves her, and I could not ask for a better match. I am just being sentimental tonight. When you made the announcement, I realized how quickly the time has flown between

193

her birth and this day. And there are Eddie and Vi, the twins, Rosemary, and Danny. Our time with them all seems so brief. The day will come for each of them to leave the nest and take wing."

"And each of them will fly straight and true, though our adventurous Vi may fly farther than the rest for her happiness. That is what we are working for, my love, to prepare each one of our fledglings to grow into eagles. That is the hope of all parents, isn't it? To see their children grow in the ways of our Lord and carry His message on in their own lives and to the next generation."

Elsie squeezed Edward's hand affectionately. "Of all the things I hope to accomplish in this life," she said, "that is my greatest hope — to share my love of the Lord with my children, to teach them of His goodness and His gift of salvation, to guide them in His light, and to see them flourish in His eternal love. But we shall miss Missy's presence here, you must admit."

"More than I am capable of admitting," Edward replied. "But my love and hopes for her outweigh all else. And now, my dear Wife, should we not retire for the night? A new day approaches, and our fledglings will be up early."

"Just one more look at the stars before we go inside, Edward," Elsie said. "They shine so brightly for us tonight."

Who are the Keiths?
What kind of life do they lead?
What family secrets do they hold?

Find out in:

MILLIE'S UNSETTLED SEASON

Book One of the
*A Life of Faith:
Millie Keith* Series

* Now Available as a Dramatized Audiobook!

— ABOUT THE AUTHOR —

*M*artha Finley was born on April 26, 1828, in Chillicothe, Ohio. Her mother died when Martha was quite young, and her father, James Finley, a doctor and devout Christian, soon remarried. Martha's stepmother, Mary Finley, was a kind and caring woman who always nurtured Martha's desire to learn and supported her ambition to become a writer.

Martha was well-educated for a girl of her times. After her father's death in 1851, she began her teaching career in Indiana. She later lived with an elder sister in New York City, where Martha continued teaching and began writing stories for Sunday school children. Martha also lived in Philadelphia where her early stories were first published by the Presbyterian Publication Board, and then she worked as a teacher in Phoenixville, Pennsylvania for two years. Determined to become a full-time writer, Martha returned to Philadelphia. Even though she sold several stories (some written under the pen name of "Martha Farquharson"), her first efforts at novel-writing were not successful. But during a period of recuperation from a fall, she crafted the basics of a book that would make her one of the country's best-known and most beloved novelists.

Three years after Martha began writing Elsie Dinsmore, the story of the lonely little Southern girl was accepted by the New York firm of Dodd Mead. The publishers divided the original manuscript into two complete books; they also honored Martha's request that pansies (flowers, Martha explained, that symbolized "thoughts of you") be printed on the books' covers. Released in 1868, Elsie Dinsmore became the publisher's best-selling book that year, launching a series that sold millions of copies at home and abroad.

The Elsie stories eventually expanded to twenty-eight volumes and included the lives of Elsie's children and grandchildren. Miss Finley published her final Elsie novel in 1905. Four years later, she died less than three months before her eighty-second birthday. She is buried in Elkton, Maryland, where she lived for more than thirty years in the house she built with proceeds from her writing career. Her large estate, carefully managed by her youngest brother, Charles, was left to family members and charities.

Martha Finley was a remarkable woman who lived a quiet Christian life; yet through her many writings, she affected the lives of several generations of Americans for the better. She never married, never had children, yet she left behind a unique legacy of faith.